MAT WAUGH

CHEEKY CHARLIE

BUGS AND BANANAS

BOOK 2

For Mary, who twinkles still
in her granddaughters' eyes.

And for Kate, who gives everyone
reasons to smile.

Contents

Has anyone told you?

Just before I begin the stories, I want to make sure that you know about my free Charlie book, Festival. If you're yawning already, you can ignore this bit. But if you're wondering what I'm talking about, look out for a bit near the end of the book when I tell you all about it. It's a cracker, as my Dad would say, but then he talks a lot of nonsense. But then I would say it's brilliant, and you can definitely trust me.

Right, let's get started on my new stories about the cheekiest brother you've ever known!

Harry

This bit doesn't count

Hello. This is Harry, the girl with the boy's name. But please don't keep talking about that because it gets on my nerves.

This book isn't about me, even though that would be a very good book. It's about my little brother Charlie.

One more thing before we get started. If somebody is reading this chapter to you before bed, or even if you're reading it yourself, it doesn't count. It's not a real chapter, and it's not that long. So don't let anyone tell you to go to bed before the end of the first proper story. Parents can be quite sneaky. You need to watch them like a hawk.

So I'm the girl with the naughty, nutty brother: the boy everyone calls Cheeky Charlie. I should have said niffy, too: Charlie smells weird. Do you have a smelly person in your family? I bet you do, everyone does, even if it's just the person who trumps the most. In our family that's Dad, although Mum did a real stinky-dink once when she bent over.

But Charlie smells different every day. Sometimes it's wee, especially in the mornings. But he often smells of food, too: ketchup, cake mixture, carrot sticks, Mini Cheddars or even pink foam teeth.

He sometimes smells of mud. That isn't surprising because he loves digging it out of the garden and squidging it between his fingers. When he finds any worms, he strokes them and says 'There there, wormy, you OK now.'

Once he got confused and stroked the mud and squidged the worm instead. 'My worm not wiggly any more,' he said sadly. When he couldn't stroke the worm better, he ran off to bury it. And then I wondered why the telly smelled funny and found a dried up wrinkly body under the DVD player.

On his worst days, Charlie stinks like Mrs Whippy – that's my best friend Gabby's dog.

But it's not always a nasty niff. He once smelled really minty after he gave my teddy a shave. He used Dad's shaving gel and Mum's razor. I went fruit-loop: who wants a bald teddy? Mum wasn't super-happy either.

So you can usually tell what Charlie has been doing by giving him a sniff.

But if you're thinking that Charlie smells a lot because he never takes baths, you'd be really wrong. Charlie *loves* baths. He gets in with anybody who'll let him and stays there until the water has gone cold and he's all wrinkly like Granny.

He hogs the shower, too, if Mum forgets he's in there. But she doesn't do that any more, not since he blocked the plughole with his bottom so he could make a swimming pool for his monkey. Of course he didn't just make a swimming pool, he made a little waterfall too: right out of the shower and onto the floor.

If you look at the lounge ceiling you can still see a brown mark where the water dripped through onto Dad's head as he watched TV. It's as if the ceiling has done a poo and forgotten to wipe its bottom. Dad doesn't get mad often, but he was batty-bing-bong about that.

Charlie may be smelly, but he's kind and smelly. In the morning he brings Mum and Dad things he thinks they want and shoves them under their duvet while they pretend to be asleep. This morning I was cuddling Mum in bed and having a sneaky go on her phone when he came in. I watched him toddle round to Dad's side and push in a banana and a bathmat. Dad groaned.

'Daddy, snack for you!'

Dad groaned even louder. 'Thanks,' he said without opening his eyes.

'The mat is for when you do dwibbles.'

'Ugh.' Dad rolled over and shoved his face into the pillow.

Charlie gave the duvet a pat and came round to Mum's side. In went a toothbrush, some jigsaw pieces and a whisk.

'I got a toofbrush for your stinky breff Mummy,' said Charlie.

'Good thinking Batman,' grunted Dad into his pillow.

'And a puzzle to keep you busy.'

Mum reached down and pulled out the whisk. 'And what am I supposed to do with this?' she croaked. 'Or shouldn't I ask?'

'Is for pancakes. I want pancakes for beckfast.'

'Ooh yes, I'd like pancakes too please Mum!' I added. 'Charlie, how do you ask nicely?' I reminded him.

'Peas. PEAS! I WANT PANCAKE PEAS!' Charlie shouted.

Mum and Dad both groaned at exactly the same time and pulled the duvet up over their heads.

I planned to stop here and start the stories. But then I thought you should know that Charlie gives things to *everyone*.

So before we begin, let me tell you about last week. After we'd helped Mum with her shopping, she took us to a café. It's my favourite because they sell amazing cupcakes with *loads* of icing on them. Sometimes there's more icing than cake.

Because we'd been extra good, Mum said we could have a cake each. I chose a chocolate sponge with white icing and sprinkles. Charlie chose a red one with vanilla icing that even ran down the sides.

'Are you sure, Charlie? You didn't like that one last time,' asked Mum.

Charlie nodded and started panting like a dog.

'OK. I'll believe you, though I don't know why. As long as you don't waste it.'

How do you eat your cakes? I've got a brilliant way. You take off the wrapper and nibble all the cake from underneath until it is just icing. And… smoosh! You mush your teeth into it. If you're lucky, you get a sugar shiver.

Mum's phone rang.

'What?' she said. 'You're very quiet.' She looked at her phone as if that would help her hear better.

'Hang on. Nope, didn't get that. Listen, I'm going outside. Hold on a second.'

She covered the phone with her hand. 'You're in charge,' she said to me. 'Behave.'

Mum glanced across to a smartly dressed granddad on the next table who was sipping a cup of tea. 'I'm sorry, would you mind keeping an eye on these two while I take this call?'

'I'd be delighted,' he said in a surprised, posh voice like the Queen, but a man. 'I'm sure they won't give me any trouble.'

Mum raised her eyebrows at me.

'I'm in charge,' I told him.

'I'm sure you are,' said the man. 'I'll be your staff sergeant. You tell me if there's any trouble in the ranks.'

Well there wasn't any trouble in the ranks, whatever they are, because it's hard to cause trouble when your mouth is full of cake.

Charlie got down from his chair. 'You wan some?' he asked the man.

'Goodness no, I can't take rations from a private.'

'Is cake, not rations,' said Charlie. 'Is for you.'

'No, no, I couldn't. Though… it does look mighty fine.'

'Go on take it,' said Charlie, pushing his plate across the table. 'Mummy says I not to waste it.'

'Charlie,' I said, 'I don't think –'

'Well your Mummy is right, of course. Tell you what, why don't you leave it there, young chap,' said the old man. He gazed at the cake and his eyes went all misty.

Charlie reached out and pulled the plate back towards him. 'No. I not doing it. How you ask nicely?' asked Charlie, rolling his eyes.

'I beg your pardon?' said the man. He raised his eyebrows in surprise at being told off by someone who could hardly see over the table. And then he realised what Charlie meant. 'Oh, yes, ah, *thank you*, young man.'

Charlie shook his head, his curly hair wobbling. 'Is not right. You say the magic word.'

'Errm, please? Or both – thank you please?'

Charlie nodded and pushed the plate back.

The man sighed, broke off a chunk of cake and popped it into his mouth. Although it didn't have any icing, I think he got a sugar shiver too. He closed his eyes, smiled and reached for more.

At that moment Mum came back. 'Everything OK?' she asked us. 'Thanks for looking after them.'

'No problem at all,' he said when he'd finished his mouthful, 'in fact the youngster insisted I eat your spare cake. I feel rather bad now, I do hope that's OK.'

'What? Yes, of course, that's fine,' said Mum, a bit confused. She sat down.

'What spare cake?' she whispered to me.

'It was Charlie's,' I said. 'He didn't want the cakey bit.'

Charlie was now trying to balance a spoon on the end of his nose.

Crumbs were falling from the old man's mouth as he pushed in big pieces of cake. He noticed Mum and me spying on him, pretended to salute, and rubbed his tummy.

'Charlie… what happened to the icing on your cake?' asked Mum, peering at the piece on the man's plate.

'I ate it,' said Charlie, dropping the spoon on the floor.

'I see. And how did you take the icing off?'

'I licked it off,' came Charlie's voice from under the table.

'You… licked it off. And then you gave the cake to the gentleman.'

'Yes!' Charlie came out with the spoon hanging from his nose. 'I use lots of lick to make it clean all over. Hey, look at my spoony nose!'

Mum covered her face with her hands.

'Shall I tell the man?' I asked, getting out of my seat.

'No! Definitely not,' she whispered, pulling me down. She smiled over at him. 'Come on, let's go.'

Mum shoved everything into the pushchair quickly. 'Good bye!' she said in a cheery voice as we passed the man's table.

'Cheerio!' he said. He cupped his hand to his face so he could do one of those loud whispers that everyone can hear. Why do grown-ups do that? 'What a kind boy you have there, a real credit to you,' he said to Mum. She half-smiled.

'And what a delicious cake, too. I thought it might be a bit dry, but in fact it was deliciously moist.'

So here's how this book works. I want to tell you lots of stories about Charlie. They're all piled up higgledy-piggledy in my head, they just need me to sort them out and write them down.

But have you ever tried to write a long story? It takes ages. And I don't get much time because I have dance club and football club and film club, and I need to play with my best friend Maryam.

But in the gaps, and when Dad makes me turn the iPad off, I'll tell you what Charlie's been doing: and you won't *believe* some of it. I'm surprised Charlie hasn't been arrested. I would arrest him. Every day.

Right, let's begin. Get ready, here comes Charlie!

Ferry

'There's a hole in the boat!'

Charlie leaned forward in his car seat to get a better view of the ferry in front of us. We were in a queue of cars, waiting to board.

'Hole! Hole! Hole! The boat will sink!' he shrieked. Then, in a normal voice: 'I want my armbands.'

'It's not a boat, it's a ferry,' I said. 'And the hole is where you drive in.'

'Daddy going to drive in the sea,' said Charlie. 'He always crashes.'

'Oi!' said Dad. 'I have only crashed once. And that crash, my little tinker, was *not* my fault. In fact, since this car seat is still stained from the muck you tipped all over me, I'd say you were a little bit to blame.'

He's talking about a journey last year when Charlie did his pointing thing. Charlie doesn't point like a normal person. Normal people like you and me lift our hands and put our fingers out and say 'Wow, what a pretty flower!' or 'Why does that dog have three legs?'

But not Charlie. He *throws* his hand out like he's throwing an invisible frisbee. He jumps up and down and shouts, and you can never tell what he's pointing at because his arm waggles all over the place, and you can't understand a word he says.

Anyway, Charlie had been travelling in the front, strapped into his car seat. Dad had taken Charlie and me to IKEA and bought some big long furniture, so Dad needed to move the seats around so we would all fit.

The crash happened when Charlie noticed a pink car. But he had forgotten that he had a drink in his hand. When he pointed the lid came off and the drink spurted all over Dad. Dad shouted something like 'Aaarf!' and crashed into the car in front of him at the traffic lights. A woman got out and shouted at Dad through the car window. Dad sat in his seat staring straight ahead, with strawberry McFlurry dripping off his eyebrows.

But that was all last year. Today we were going on holiday and driving onto the ferry. Inside it was dark and there was a nasty, oily smell. Men in orange jackets were waving and shouting, and we drove so far I thought we would come out of the other end and plop into the sea like Charlie said.

But eventually we came to a stop, right at the front of a line of cars.

'That's a result, we'll drive off first,' said Dad. 'That's assuming I can get my enormous belly down the stairs after my gut-buster breakfast.'

'No need,' said Mum. 'I've got jam sandwiches for everyone in the change bag, and lots of water.'

Dad turned round and made a face at us. 'So I planned to have bacon, sausage, egg, beans, mushrooms, black pudding and chips. But now I'm going to have a jam sarnie and water. I think I'm on the wrong holiday.'

Whack! Mum hit him on the head with the road map.

'Ah well, I suppose Mummy's right, as always. Everybody ready? Right my little funsters, let's go!'

We got out. Mum grabbed our jackets and jumpers, the change bag, extra snacks, a pile of paper and a box of crayons, the camera, her purse and sunglasses, a blanket, Charlie's sun hat, our tickets and some other stuff. Dad took his wallet and his phone. We clomped our way up the stairs with the other passengers.

When we got to the passenger deck we found ourselves next to the information desk. We stopped to look at the map.

'Now don't forget, we came up using the red staircase, so we should –' said Mum. But it's a mystery what else she said because the lady on the information desk made an announcement over the ship's loudspeakers.

'Ladies and gentlemen, welcome on board. On our ship today you'll find blah blah blah… '

She didn't actually say 'blah blah', that's what you say in stories to show that the woman was talking a lot, but I wasn't listening to the real words.

Mum waited until she'd finished. 'So that's the red staircase we need to remember,' she continued. 'Now, who'd like to –'

But we didn't hear the rest, because the information lady had something else to say.

'You'll also discover a wide variety of ladies' perfumes, electronic devices, chocolate and snacks, all available in our duty free shop.'

'A booty free shop!' said Charlie, who had definitely heard that bit, and started to run. Dad picked him up by the armpits and his little legs carried on running like Scooby Doo.

'Not so fast, sailor boy,' said Dad, 'there's nothing free in a *duty* free shop.'

'She said free!' said Charlie.

'Yes, but –'

'That naughty. Is naughty to say fibs, isn't it Mummy?'

'Yes, darling. Naughty woman. Now as I was saying, if we went to the –'

But you won't believe this: the information lady smiled at her and started talking again.

Blah-de-blah blah. I can't even be bothered to tell you what she said it was so boring.

Charlie stood next to Mum, wanting to tell her something. Mum put her finger on her lips and pointed at the information lady. Charlie frowned, turned around, and marched right up to the desk. The lady barely glanced at him.

'Is *rude*,' said Charlie at the top of his voice.

'Mummy talking.' He started stamping.

'You.' *(left foot stamp)*

'Have.' *(right foot stamp)*

'To.' *(left foot stamp)*

'Wait!' *(left right stamp, with podgy fists pumping up and down in front of him)*

And then he marched back to Mum and put his arm around her leg.

The lady stared at us for a long time before switching on her microphone. 'Please can I remind parents to keep their children under control at all times,' she announced. She did a little smile at us but she didn't mean it. You could tell because she crinkled her face up like a crisp packet but her eyes didn't go shiny.

'I know when we're not wanted,' said Mum, pushing us down the corridor towards the café. 'Did you see her miserable face?'

'She looks like someone dropped a stink bomb down her pants,' I said.

'For once, I agree with you,' said Mum, and she took my hand.

As soon as we found a free table Charlie crawled straight under it like he always does. He squeezed between our knees, pulled at the chair legs and banged his head on the table.

'Ouch, is hurty,' came a voice. 'I done a hole in my head, my brain is squiggling out.'

We ignored him, and he carried on exploring.

One minute later, another cry. 'I finded money!'

Now that sounded more interesting. I took a squizz under the table. Charlie was clutching a shiny 20p coin.

'I buy a rabbit,' he said, 'or a smellycopter. Where I put it, Mummy?'

I got that funny burning feeling in my tummy, the one you get when someone else gets something you want. I'm saving for roller boots. I wished I'd found the money.

'Mummy, where I put it? Mummy? Mummy, where I put it? Mummy? Mummy?'

He droned on and on and on. He does that until he gets an answer, and sometimes that takes ages because Mum is too busy eating Mini Cheddars. I think the crunching sound stops her ears working.

Charlie crawled out, still asking, still holding his shiny 20p. He bumped headfirst into Dad who was crouching down, searching for more snacks in the change bag. You could see Dad's underpants, and even part of his bottom. That often happens. Maybe his undies are the wrong size.

Charlie held his 20p tightly and made his thinking face.

'I put it in Daddy's piggyback,' he said. And he reached out and slotted it into Dad's bottom crack!

'Oi!' shouted Dad. He tried to get up. He banged his head on the table, too.

'Ouch! And what the devil was that?' He started jiggling around and shoving his hand down his trousers. The children on the next table started giggling and pointing at him.

'Are you doing a dance?' said Charlie. 'I good at dancing.' And he put his arms out and flapped them like a chicken.

'Whatever you've put down there, it's stuck right where the sun doesn't shine,' said Dad. He eventually pulled the 20p out of his bottom and held it out to Charlie.

'Ugh, I bet that smells pooey,' I said.

'Wrong. My bottom is squeaky clean,' said Dad. 'You could eat your dinner off it, except your sausages might roll off.'

'It is *way* too early for all this botty talk,' said Mum, grabbing the coin and giving it a rub with a wet wipe. 'Here you go Charlie, stick this somewhere safe.'

Charlie stuffed the coin into his little trouser pocket, and we had our snack.

After we'd finished, Mum told me that we could go anywhere we liked as long as I looked after Charlie, and as long as we didn't go outside or up or down any stairs. So we went exploring.

Have you ever been on a ferry? It's brilliant when there are big waves because the floor tilts and you go 'wa-hey' and stagger from side to side and sometimes you even fall over. There weren't many big waves this time, but we pretended there were.

We soon found the playroom. These are usually a bit rubbish, and this one definitely was: there were lots of those squishy coloured cubes, and a telly showing baby cartoons. But Charlie loved it, of course, and he started piling up the cubes and trying to climb on top.

'I do four!' he shouted to me as he climbed on top of a pile of three cubes and fell straight off again. (He's not good at counting.)

'Now I do five!' he said, starting to stack them up again. The other children moved away from him nervously.

I wandered up the corridor. Next to the playroom I found something Dad told me is called an arcade, with fruit machines. Do you know what I'm talking about? Fruit machines are covered in lights and buttons, and pictures that spin round. There are loads of them in service stations.

Of course when Charlie first found out that they're called fruit machines he thought you could get *narnas* out of it or even *store berries*. But Dad told him that you put money in, and sometimes you get money out, but mostly you don't, and that only grown-ups can play. I sometimes wonder if grown-ups are clever, because that sounds silly to me.

Next to the arcade I found windows with a view right out to sea and I watched the other ferries as we crossed paths. Some people were waving at me from another boat. I had no idea who they were, so I didn't wave back.

I must have been there for quite a while because when I remembered Charlie, he had gone. Disappeared, like an ice cube in your mouth.

He'd probably returned to Mum, so I ran back to the café.

Uh-oh: no sign of him.

'Mummeeee,' I said. 'I –'

'Where's Charlie?' she said, straight away. Dad lowered his phone.

'Well I was ferry-spotting out of the window and he wandered off! It's his fault, I didn't know he'd run away!'

'Don't worry, I'll find him,' said Dad. 'The little tyke is probably eating a poor trucker's breakfast. I'll sniff out trouble, he'll be there. Come on Harry, you're on Search and Rescue duty with me.'

That's why I love Dad. Anything can be a game. He once used his phone to time how long it takes me to have a poo. (The answer was two minutes, including wiping and washing hands, but I'm sure I could do it quicker.) Another time he bet that I couldn't fit a whole bowlful of jelly into my mouth at once. I said I could, so I spooned it in, more and more, squishing it into my cheeks. But I pushed a bit too hard and started coughing, and blobs of red jelly sprayed all over Dad and Charlie. It went in their hair and everything. He had to say sorry a lot after that, but I didn't because it wasn't my fault.

Now what was I talking about? You shouldn't let me tell you other stuff halfway through, it's confusing. Oh yes, that time on the ferry, when we lost Charlie. So we set off, half-walking, half-running down the corridors, searching for him.

Not in the playroom. Not in the arcade. Not by the windows. Not in the other café. Not by the toilets.

'He can't be too far,' said Dad, 'because they lock the doors to the car deck, and he's too small to open any others.' But he did look a bit worried.

We turned a corner; there weren't many people around in this bit. Then another corner, another corridor. At the far end of the next corridor and vanishing out of sight was Charlie's can't-miss-it curly hair. It had to be him, except he was holding a lady's hand – and it wasn't Mum. She was wearing a blue jacket and skirt with her bobbly hair twirled up on top of her head with a purple ribbon to hold it up.

'Charlie!' I shouted, but Dad had already spotted him. He grabbed my hand and we sprinted after them.

Now, I have a question. Has anyone talked to you about strangers yet? In school, or at home? If not, they will soon, I bet. Mrs Schofield told us. She said that if a person you don't know asks you to do something, like if they want you to help them find their doggy, or they want to give you cola bottles, then you need to check with someone else that it's OK.

'But what if I can't find anyone that I know?' I had asked.

'Brilliant question, Harry, well done,' said Mrs Schofield. My cheeks burned red hot.

'In that case you should ask someone in a shop, or a bus driver, or a lollipop lady, or even knock on someone's door if you're worried.'

'Oh,' I said, and we ran out to play.

The reason I'm asking you is because Charlie hasn't had the stranger-danger talk yet. Or if he did, he didn't listen to a word of it because here he was, walking along with a strange lady on a boat!

So we followed them, like super spies.

Just as we were about to catch up with them, they were gone. But this time we knew where to look because the strange lady pushed a few buttons on a keypad and took Charlie through a door with a big blue sign that said 'CREW ONLY'.

Dad tried the door. No luck. He thumped on the door and starting shouting. 'Oi! Open up!' Thump thump. 'Charlie, can you hear me?' Thump thump.

'Daddy! Where *are* you?'

That was Charlie, of course, but his voice sounded loud – much louder than you'd expect through a door. I peered around the corner of the corridor. We were right back at the information desk, and who did we find sitting on top of it like a garden gnome? Charlie!

'Daddy, he's here!' I said.

Dad stopped thumping the door and came round the corner. 'Oh. I am *so* sorry,' he said to the lady with the purple ribbon. 'I never let him out of my sight, I'm not sure how it happened.'

Purple ribbon lady smiled. 'No problem, sir, I have a little chap about the same age. He's always doing a vanishing act.' Then, appearing from behind purple ribbon lady as if she'd been hiding in her shadow, the rude woman stepped forward: the one who'd interrupted Mum. 'We would ask that you keep your children nearby though, sir.' She wrinkled her nose at Charlie.

'Well I'll certainly bear your wishes in mind,' said Dad in a scratchy voice, the one he uses before he gets a bit shouty.

'I just need you to sign an incident form and provide ID before you reclaim your child,' said rude woman. 'One second, I'll get the paperwork,' and she disappeared into a room behind the desk.

'You have *got* to be joking,' muttered Dad.

Ribbon lady smiled and put her arm around Charlie who was still sitting on the information desk.

'Bon voyage, young man,' she said, and turned to Dad. 'I'm sure you'll be finished here soon.' And she opened the door to the corridor and vanished.

Dad's phone rang. That's what you say when phones make a noise, isn't it, but it's a silly word because it doesn't ring. Dad's phone sounds like a cow mooing, which drives Mum nuts. He said he chose it because it makes him feel like a farmer, and that's about right because our house is a pigsty with lots of dirty animals running around. I think he's being rude about Charlie and Mum.

Anyway, he answered his cow phone and started to tell Mum what had happened, wandering over to a window as he spoke.

Charlie was still sitting up on the desk, bored. And when Charlie gets bored, his hands start prodding, poking, and fiddling with anything that's handy. Like the rude lady's microphone.

'Say something funny,' I whispered to Charlie.

Charlie leaned over and started talking into the microphone, but of course it didn't work.

'Hello hello hello,' he said. He leaned closer. 'My name is Charlie I am free.' He leaned a bit more and put out his hand to stop himself falling over. A loud scrunchy sound made me jump.

'I do smelly trumps,' he said.

That confused me: Charlie was in front of me of course, but his voice also seemed to be around us, too. I pushed myself up onto my tiptoes: Charlie was leaning on the talk button!

Charlie grinned at me with a proper ten-out-of-ten cheeky face. He looked down at his fat little hand, pressed the microphone button and giggled. Laughter bubbled out from behind me, from the left, the right and everywhere else.

The corridors were empty. Nobody ran up to tell us off and Dad was still talking on his cow phone.

I know I should have said something. I knew it at the time. I should stop Charlie, I thought, or call Dad. But... well, would you? No, neither did I.

'Say something about the shop!' I whispered.

'Free perfume for smelly ladies in the... the... the... ' Charlie, announced, getting stuck.

'Duty free shop!' I whispered.

'Booty free shop. And free daddy juice for firsty daddies,' he said, enjoying himself.

Uh-oh: a man carrying a newspaper appeared round a corner. He'd definitely seen us: he had a big grin on his face. But can you guess what he did? He winked at Charlie, gave me a thumbs up, and walked right past!

Charlie didn't need my help any more. 'Free chips for boys in the café!' he continued. I pinched his leg.

'OI!' he shouted, and his voice came from every corner, like when you walk under a bridge and you make 'woo-wooo!' sound of a train.

'OK and free chips for girls, but not dip-dip.'

Suddenly, about a million things happened.

Dad started striding towards us, his phone still pressed to his ear, yelling, 'Charlie, get away from there!'

The corridor echoed with the sound of thumping, thundering feet and a herd of shouty children ran past. You know what it's like when they do a cake sale at school, and everyone runs around and gets excited? It was like that.

'Free chips!' shouted one little boy as he ran, and he did a little punch in the air.

At the same time the grumpy woman burst back through the door behind the desk. But if she was grumpy before, now she was *furious*. She screwed up her face until her eyes became shiny little black spots, like currants on a gingerbread man. She took a big step forward and grabbed Charlie under the armpits and put him down on the floor.

But I've told you before, Charlie doesn't let go easily, and he hadn't finished yet.

'Get off me!' he said, wriggling to get away, and

still holding the microphone. Although I couldn't see him, his voice was still booming out from all the speakers on the ferry. 'You a very rude lady.'

'Give me that microphone, you little wotsit,' she screeched, trying to sound scary, although I'm not sure anyone is afraid of being called a cheesy crisp.

Dad had run to the door around the corner and jiggled the door handle again. It was still locked, of course, so he came running back. He tried to reach over and grab Charlie but his arms weren't long enough, so he climbed over the desk, grunting, with his pants showing and everything. I gave his bottom a push, like he does to me when I can't get over a gate.

Dad pulled Charlie away from the lady. 'Hey hey, there's no need for that, either of you!' said Dad, carrying him high up over the desk.

'Mushrooms is fifty pounds,' said the ship's speakers. Charlie was still clutching the microphone while the woman was jumping up, trying to grab it off him.

'Cabbage is sixty twenty pounds. And stinky fish is a million-ty pounds because it's yucky. And –'

'Put it down. Now,' said Dad, pulling the microphone out of Charlie's hands. After a loud click, the scrunchy microphone sound stopped.

'Charlie, you're in BIG TROUBLE,' said Dad in captial letters. 'You need to say sorry.'

Charlie reached out and grabbed the microphone and put his thumb on the button. 'I very sorry.'

'Not into the microphone!' said Dad, snatching it back and putting it on the desk, well out of Charlie's reach.

'Sir, I ask that you stay here while I alert the captain,' said the woman, reaching for a phone. I very much doubt Charlie's microphone takeover was going to be news to the captain, unless he had socks in his ears.

'Not bloomin' likely,' said Dad, grabbing our hands and pulling us away into the corridor. 'You were asking for that.'

An old lady with white hair and a big smile reached out from a bench and put her hand on Charlie's arm, making us all jump. It was as if part of the ship had come to life, but I realised she was wearing a yellow dress that matched the colour of the wall.

'That's the funniest thing I've seen all holiday,' she said. She'd been sitting there all the time, observing us. 'But you lot should make yourselves scarce. I think you might have caused a mutiny.'

She winked at Dad and waved her walking stick towards the café. Sure enough, a big crowd of children had gathered around a waiter, shouting and pointing at the speaker on the wall. 'Free chips! They said free chips! We want free chips!' they were shouting.

'What's a moo tinny?' said Charlie, as Dad tugged us away from the crowd.

'It's when a trouble-maker gets out of hand,' said Dad, 'which is exactly what just happened. And Harry, you're for the high jump too, when Mummy gets hold of you.' That didn't sound good.

'I can jump high,' said Charlie, who did a little skip as he walked.

'Mummy!' he shouted as we approached. And do you know what else happened? As soon as Mum spotted Dad, she started laughing. He started laughing. Charlie made his eyes go wonky and rocked from side to side, which he does when he's giddy. I started laughing too because they weren't that cross. I love my Mum and Dad.

A little later, after I'd run up and down the corridors a bit more and complained about how boring it was, Mum asked me to fetch Charlie because it was nearly time to get off.

But Charlie had disappeared again. Poof! There weren't any puffs of smoke of course, but he had definitely evaporated. I checked behind all the toys in the playroom, although there weren't many coloured cubes left any more. Mum would kill me if I'd lost him again.

I spotted him. Inside the arcade, next to a fruit machine stood a tall, wobbly pile of squishy cubes. The stack of six was leaning against the machine, but even so it waved and tipped all over the place like an Eiffel tower made of jelly. And that wasn't surprising because right at the top, with his arms stretched high, sat Charlie. And in his sausage fingers was his shiny 20p coin.

'Charlie!' I shouted, and I started to run.

At the same time, coming from the opposite direction, strode Dad. 'Charlie-boy!' he yelled, and he started to run, too.

What happened next is a bit weird. Have you watched any slow motion stuff on telly, or maybe on a phone? Like when those Slo-Mo men try to pop a giant water balloon by jumping on it out of a tree? You should definitely find that one on YouTube, it's *brilliant*. Anyway, this was like the Slo-Mo guys but in real life, because even though I was running, it seemed to take ages to happen.

First, the red cube near the bottom popped out like an escaping strawberry, and so all the other cubes on top started to topple over. And since he was balancing on top of those, Charlie started to fall, too.

Charlie made this crazy sound, like a cat pretending to be a ghost: 'Yawwww-ooooo-wooo!' And as he shouted, he pushed himself in one last big jump towards the machine.

Now remember this is my brother we're talking about. If you throw him a ball it goes straight through his hands and lands on his feet, and he does a clap about ten minutes later to show he was trying to catch it. He puts his shoes on the wrong way round. He can't do up a zip, or buttons. He's basically a bit rubbish.

But not this time. Because in slooooooooow

motion, his hand reached out and pushed that shiny 20p right into the slot in the machine! Straight away, all the lights started flashing and the fruit machine started playing a tune: 'bloople bloople blippety blippety blink blink blop!'

The cubes had fallen to the ground now. But Charlie hadn't: he was hopping up and down, trampling on the bit with the buttons, trying to find something to hold. And while he did this the machine went crazy, with pictures spinning and numbers lighting up. Perhaps it didn't like being trodden on by chubby boys.

'Hold on Charlie!' shouted Dad.

'Hold on Charlie!' I repeated, in case Charlie didn't hear Dad.

But it was all too slippery for Charlie. Just as I was arriving, his balancing act ended. As he fell his bottom landed on the biggest button with a *whumpf!* He bounced off, landing flat on his back on top of the scattered cubes.

I ran up to Charlie, expecting him to be crying like a baby. But I should have known better. Although he had his hands over his face, he was laughing like a drain. (I've always thought that a drain is a silly thing to compare a laugh to, but my teacher says it's a good simile so I'm including it here in case it gets me on the Proud Cloud on Monday.)

At the same time that Charlie landed on the cubes a siren started blaring out. 'Nee-naw nee-naw!', like a police car. And another noise, too: a big, metal 'Ker-thunk! Ker-thunk! Ker-thunk!' sound.

Guess what? There were coins *binging* out of the fruit machine! And this was proper money, too, not 2 pees or 5 pees, but lots and lots of shiny pound coins.

'What on earth...?' said Dad, as he arrived, huffing and puffing like Thomas and his Friends.

'I making money Daddy!' said Charlie, who'd jumped to his feet, and was now swishing his hands in the coins.

The machine didn't stop. 'Ker-thunk! Ker-thunk!' All the lights were flashing, including a big sign at the top saying 'JACKPOT!'

By now, lots of people had stopped.

'Nice one buddy!' shouted a fat man with a flowery shirt and one of those bottom bags you wear round your waist. He reached over the cubes and held up his hand to Dad for a high five.

Dad looked confused, but slapped his hand. 'Oh, erm, yeah, thanks very much,' he said.

The fat man turned to me. 'Here's hoping he spends it on you, Lady Luck!' he boomed, even though he was close enough for me to smell his coffee breath. He held up his hand and since I liked this idea a lot, I gave him an extra slappy high five, the sort that makes your hand go hot.

With one final 'ker-thunk!' the machine stopped pushing out money, the siren stopped too. Silence returned, and all the people who had stopped to find out what was going on started to drift away.

'Charlie, Charlie,' said Dad, grinning. He started taking big handfuls of money, shoving them into the pockets of his trousers. 'My boy with the Midas touch. How the *devil* are we going to explain this to Mummy?'

'I know. We buy a polar bear teddy from the shop,' said Charlie. 'And a stinky bomb for the rude lady.'

'That, my little lucky charm, is the best idea you've had all day,' said Dad. And with a polar bear roar he picked us up, one under each arm, and ran off down the corridor with his bulging pockets going clickety-clink, clinkety-clink.

Dinner Time

'Your tea's on the table, Harry, so please come downstairs as soon as you're ready thank you very much!'

That's what Dad *should* have shouted. But instead he yelled, 'Harry, your tea's ready NOW! If you don't get your big fat bottom down these stairs in three seconds, I'm throwing your tea in the bin!'

There were three reasons why I didn't answer.

Number one, he should be more polite than that.

Number two, I was sitting in my room making a bracelet for my best friend Kiana.

And number three, I was sticking my tongue out which I do whenever I'm concentrating, and you can't talk when your tongue is sticking out.

It's impossible. Try it now. Go on: say 'What's for tea?'

See? I told you, it's impossible, you sound like a dog pretending to talk.

The shouty monster downstairs was back. 'Harry… get down here now. I mean it!'

One more bead to go… Oh. I dropped it. It pinged off somewhere into the carpet fur. How annoying. That was definitely Dad's fault.

'OK OK I'm COMING!' I shouted back. Seriously, what is his problem? I hope your Mum and Dad aren't like that.

By the time I got down to the kitchen everyone else was already there: Mum, Dad, Charlie and Uncle Mike, who had come for a sleepover.

Do you have an uncle? Uncle Mike is definitely my favourite uncle. I only have one uncle. (Try saying 'uncle' ten times very fast. Isn't it a funny word?)

'Hey there Prince Harry,' said Uncle Mike. He always calls me that. So I punched him on the arm as hard as I could as I walked past. I always do that. He pretends it doesn't hurt because he's so big and tough, but I know it does.

Now you might be wondering about Charlie

since these stories are all about him. For once he was doing what he should: sitting in his chair, waiting nicely for his dinner.

Well I say nicely, but that's only true if you think it's nice to put your pointing finger so far up your nose it looks as if you've got a hand growing out of your face. He waggled his finger about and that seemed to be controlling his eyes because they were wiggling around too.

'Have you found anything good up there?' asked Uncle Mike. 'Cheesy puffs? The TV remote? A hamster, maybe?'

Charlie pulled his finger out. Attached to the end was a massive crusty bogey, and attached to *that* was a long, gluey, shiny, stretchy string of snot that swung around in the air as he waved his hand.

'That's top notch,' said Uncle Mike.

'That's gross,' I said, though secretly I was quite impressed: my stringers are never that big.

'Hey! I catched a big one!' said Charlie, chuckling.

Mum, who was helping Dad in the kitchen, glanced across. 'No thank you, Charlie, that's disgusting.'

'Sorreeee!' said Charlie. 'I put it back.' And

he pushed his finger back up his nose. The silvery rope of snot slapped against his cheek and stayed there, like a snail had crawled over his face.

'Double gross,' I said.

'You're a classy little dude, aren't you?' said Uncle Mike.

'Incoming!' shouted Dad, throwing a packet of wet wipes across the room to Uncle Mike. Without taking his eyes off Charlie he reached up and caught them. I told you, Uncle Mike is great.

'What's for tea?' I asked.

'Roast chicken,' said Dad.

Yummy. That's my favourite. Apart from jacket potato, pizza, cherry yoghurts, chips, pasta and ham sandwiches.

'I luf chickens. Bock bock bock,' said Charlie, flapping his arms while Uncle Mike wiped the slime off his face. 'Can we play wiv it after? We can chase it in the garden!'

'This chicken doesn't want to play any more,' said Dad as he put a bowl of chicken pieces in the middle of the table.

'Is he a bit tired?' said Charlie. 'Maybe he needs a lie down.'

'I think like he's already having one of those,'

said Uncle Mike. 'All over the plate.'

'Now now, boys,' said Mum, bringing across massive bowls of roast potatoes and vegetables. 'I'm not sure who's teasing who here, but it's time to change the subject.'

'Charlie,' said Mum, 'tell Uncle Mike what we did this morning.'

'I look for hugs,' said Charlie. 'In the park.'

'Hugs? In the park?' said Uncle Mike, like an echo. His eyebrows rose so far they nearly disappeared into his hair. 'Well… that's cool, I guess. Did you get any?'

'Yes!' said Charlie. 'I finded some hugs in the grass, under stones and some in my pants too!'

Uncle Mike turned to Mum as she sat down. She grinned. 'Bugs, Charlie, not hugs. We went on a bug hunt.'

'Is what I said. A hug bunt,' said Charlie. His hand sneaked out towards the roast potatoes, but Dad used his lightning skills and grabbed his podgy fist before he reached the bowl. Charlie made a face.

'It was great,' I said. 'Charlie put loads of bugs into a Tic Tac box so they would have a party.'

'Do bugs eat Tic Tacs?' asked Uncle Mike.

'It was empty,' said Charlie. 'I eated them all.'

'You ate all the bugs? That's a bit weird,' said Uncle Mike.

'No! I ate the Tic Tacs, you silly billy.'

'Watch it, Charlie,' said Mum as she served the chicken. 'No need to be cheeky.'

'I *not* cheeky, I telling Uncle Mike,' said Charlie. 'And also I made the lid open so they can breathe and I put some grass in, and I put it in my pocket. But they all run away,' he said sadly.

'Ah,' said Uncle Mike. 'And let me take a wild guess here. Is that when you found some bugs in your pants?'

'Yes!' said Charlie, and he clapped his hands together. 'I found free in my nappy pants. I fink they like it when I do trumps, coz it feels all warm.'

Mum groaned. 'That's enough already!' she said. 'Would you give it a rest with all the bottom talk, just for ten minutes?'

'She's right,' said Dad. 'We should take a botty break. No-one's allowed to say a word about Charlie's bottom.'

'Definitely. Let's put a cork in it,' said Uncle Mike, holding up the cork from the wine bottle.

Charlie's eyes widened in confusion. 'Put a cork? In my bottom?'

'Good idea. Or perhaps we should put a sock in it instead,' said Dad.

'What about a wind sock?' said Uncle Mike.

I giggled like crazy, even though I didn't completely understand. Mind you, Charlie didn't understand at all. He kept saying 'Eh? Eh? Eh? Eh?' and waving his hands around. Dad and Uncle Mike gave each other high fives.

'Aaargh!' shouted Mum, pressing her hands against her ears. 'Stop the bus, I want to get off! I want to live with a normal family!'

'I not on the bus! I not got a ticket! I *is* normal! I don't want you to go!' cried Charlie.

Mum calmed down. 'Charlie, I'm not going anywhere. It's an expression. I'm stuck with you loonies but I'm hungry, and this food is getting cold. Now has everybody got everything they need?'

'Nearly there. How many carrots do you want, Charlie?' said Dad, putting them one by one onto his plate.

'Yuck. Don't like carrots,' said Charlie.

'Rubbish,' said Dad. 'You love them. You ate a field-full last week. Do you want four or five?'

'Don't want carrots,' said Charlie, pushing them off his plate onto the table.

'Come on rabbit features, you can't eat chicken without carrots,' said Dad.

'Yes I can,' said Charlie. 'Look.' And he reached out, grabbed a piece of chicken, and stuffed it into his mouth. 'See?'

'Hmm,' said Dad.

'You asked for that,' said Uncle Mike. 'I love carrots.' He dropped them back on Charlie's plate. 'Did you know they're a superfood? They give you super powers.'

'They make you see in the dark,' I said. 'Everyone knows that.'

'True,' said Uncle Mike. 'But not many people know they also make you run faster.'

'Do they really?' I said. You have to check with Uncle Mike because he often makes up stuff.

'Oh yes,' he said, helping himself to a massive

spoonful. 'All the fastest runners in the world also eat carrots. And that's not a coincidence.'

'I like running fast,' said Charlie, and he picked up a carrot and took a bite.

'Job done,' said Dad, winking at Uncle Mike. 'Right, has everyone got everything they need?'

'Can I have gravy please Daddy,' I said. 'Just on the meat.' Dad poured it all over my food, including the broccoli, but that didn't matter because I wasn't going to eat that anyway. I don't like broccoli. My best friend Alanna says it makes your hair curly, but my hair is curly already.

'OK, let's start,' said Mum. 'Thanks Dad, this smells delicious.'

'Cheers everyone,' said Uncle Mike, and we all clinked our glasses and cups. Charlie slopped his water over the bowl of green beans, but that also didn't matter because I wasn't going to eat any of those, either. Do you like them? It's like eating hot, fat grass: yuck.

We picked up our knives and forks.

'Wait!' said Charlie. 'We not done a prayer.'

'A prayer?' said Uncle Mike. 'Since when…?'

'Ah yes,' said Dad. 'It's a new thing. They do it at buggy club. Just go with the flow, believe me.'

'Right, everyone close your eyes,' said Charlie. We all smiled and I half-closed my eyes so I could still watch him. I do that in assembly, too. Do you?

Charlie climbed down off his chair, toddled round to mine and stared at me. 'CLOSE YOUR EYES POPPERLY!' he shouted, right in my face and making me jump.

'Right, no peeking. Dear God, fank you for our lovely food. Fank you for the poor people, and people in hoppital with diseases.'

'Great,' said Dad. 'Let's start.'

'I not finished! Thank you God for everyfink. Thank you for shiny princesses, thank you for Mister Maker. Thank you for my jumper... Thank you for forks, and thank you for my trumps, and –'

'That's enough prayers now, Charlie,' said Mum firmly. 'Back to your seat and let's eat.'

And so we did, and there was peace. But not for long.

Chew, chew. Munch, munch. Slurp slurp. Everyone started eating, but all we could hear was Charlie. He's a world-class messy eater. Bits of food fall out of his mouth onto his plate, or even on the floor. We watched a horse eating muesli from a bucket last week: snap. Exactly the same.

He's rubbish with drinks, too. Anything dribbly like gravy runs down onto his chin. Then he says 'Uh! Uh! Uh!' until someone fetches kitchen roll.

'I've finished,' I said. 'Can I get down now please?' I am the quickest eater in my class.

'No,' said Dad. 'You have to sit here until we're all done. Why don't you tell Uncle Mike about the bug hunt?'

'Well, we had a pad and a pencil and a magnifying glass, and we had to find all the insects on the list. I nearly got them all. I found a –'

'I tell him! I tell him!' said Charlie. 'I finded a ant, and a wood mouse, and a wood mouse friend.'

Uncle Mike scratched his head.

'You found a wood*louse*, not a wood mouse,' said Mum.

'Ah,' said Uncle Mike.

'And I put the wood louses in my box.'

'Wood*lice*,' said Mum.

'And I found an earpig –'

'Eh?' said Uncle Mike.

'Ear*wig*,' said Mum.

47

'Oh,' said Uncle Mike.

'And also I catched a baby bird,' said Charlie.

'You what?' said Uncle Mike.

'A *lady*bird,' said Mum.

'But it flowed away,' said Charlie.

'What did?' said Uncle Mike.

'The baby bird!' said Charlie. 'You listen popperly.'

'Right, yes,' said Uncle Mike, rubbing his forehead. 'Any more?'

'Oh yes, I seed a dragon.'

'Dragon*fly*,' said Mum.

'No, I didn't see it fly,' said Charlie. 'It was sitting still!'

'No, I mean you *saw* a dragon*fly*.'

'No, I didn't saw it or chop it or anyfink!' protested Charlie. 'I is kind to insects. You is very rude Mummy.' Charlie glared at her. 'But I finded other bugs too so now I can have pets at home.'

I stayed quiet. Once Charlie is talking, it's best if you think of something else until he's finished, like who is your best friend at school. My best friend is Ella.

He had finally stopped talking.

'I got 18 points,' I said. 'And a sticker.'

'That's awesome,' said Uncle Mike. 'Now tell me about –'

But now it was Mum's turn to interrupt. 'Hang on Charlie, what did you just say? You caught the other ones because you wanted pets at home?'

'Yes,' said Charlie. 'Coz you said we can't have a monkey.'

'That's a shame,' said Uncle Mike. 'I think another monkey would fit in quite well round here.'

Dad raised his eyebrows and carried on eating.

'Charlie! That was naughty!' I said. 'You were supposed to put the bugs back in the grass.'

'Wait a second Harry, I'm not finished yet,' said Mum. Now she was doing it to me! I think we'll have to have a little chat about how rude it is to interrupt people.

'So… ' Mum stopped. She didn't even know what she wanted to say!

'Where did you put the bugs?' she said finally.

'Back in the Tic Tac box! I said dat already!' Charlie shook his head. 'But don't worry Mummy, I putted my finger in the hole to stop them.'

I spotted the Tic Tac box hidden under the edge of the vegetable bowl. At the bottom of the box, where the see-through bit is, Charlie had stuffed a small clump of grass.

'So Mummy, I push my finger in the hole like dis,' said Charlie. He poked his finger into the box and waved the box around. 'But my finger went hurty. So I maked a leaf door instead to stop them running away again.'

Charlie's face fell. 'Oh. My leaf door is gone.'

'When *exactly* did you lose your leaf?' asked Mum.

'I don't know… It was on the hole when I sit down,' said Charlie, his eyes zipping everywhere. 'But now it gone. Harry, where is my leaf?'

'Seriously Charlie, why would I have your leaf?'

As we were talking, Uncle Mike was moving plates and glasses around slowly and lifting up dishes. He put out his long pointy finger and shoved it right into the pile of green beans.

'Come along, little one,' he said. And as we stared a tiny woodlouse crawled onto his finger.

Mum did a little scream and pushed her chair back from the table. I did the same.

'Dibby Doo!' said Charlie. 'It's Dibby Doo! Mummy, it's Dibby Doo! Daddy, it's Dibby Doo! Hello Dibby Doo, how are you?'

If you're thinking 'Who's Dibby Doo?', it's one of the names that Charlie gives things. He has names for everything and they change all the time. This morning, for instance, he asked for more 'moo moo whitey' on his cereal. But yesterday he asked for cornflakes and 'cow wow juice'.

So it didn't surprise me at all when he called his woodlouse Dibby Doo.

He leaned down and put his face right next to the wriggly little thing on Uncle Mike's finger. 'There there, Dibby Doo, you be OK,' he said, 'shh, shh,' like he was trying to get a baby to sleep.

Closer and closer he got until the woodlouse could have crawled from Uncle Mike's finger onto Charlie's top lip, if he'd wanted to. (I'm saying 'he', but to be honest I couldn't tell if it was a boy or a girl woodlouse.)

But this woodlouse didn't want to go anywhere because he curled up into a ball.

'Charlie, what *are* you doing?' said Dad.

'I talking to Dibby Doo,' whispered Charlie. 'He say he lost his friend Wobbly Woo. He crying.'

'Woodlice don't cry,' I said.

'Yes. Dey. Do!' said Charlie. 'Look!'

I bent closer. Woodlice are weird. They have a shell like a tiny tortoise, but it's made up of lots of different parts so that the woodlouse can wriggle and squiggle better. They're amazing, you should find woodlouse pictures on the internet.

But although they have an awesome shell and lots of wiggly legs, woodlice can't cry. I know, because by now I was leaning right in opposite Charlie, watching Dibby Doo.

Now the next thing that happened surprised everyone, including me. Do you sneeze much? I do. Sometimes I have loads of time to get ready. My nose starts to tingle. My eyes begin to close. I start to make funny noises, louder and louder: 'Hurr… hurr… HURR… A-CHOO!'

By the time the sneeze arrives I've got my hands in front of my mouth and they get sprayed with sneeze water. I'm supposed to wash it off, but how can you do that if you're at the park? So I usually go and give Mum a cuddle and secretly wipe it on her top.

But it doesn't always happen like that. Sometimes a sneeze sneaks up on me like it's playing a game of *What's the Time Mister Wolf?* It bursts out of my mouth like a party popper.

That's what happened when I was inspecting the woodlouse. It might have been something about his crazy legs, waving in different directions, all tickly. AH-CHOO! A monster sneeze exploded out of me, with zero time to get my hands up.

Did you know that it's impossible to sneeze with your eyes open? It is. You have to close them, otherwise your eyeballs would pop out, right onto the table, and roll onto the floor. Then they'd get covered in bits of Rice Krispies and fluff, even if you picked them up straight away. But it's OK, because you can't keep them open anyway.

So when I sneezed, I closed my eyes. And when I opened them again, Dibby Doo was gone.

I looked down at the table. Nothing there. I looked at Charlie. Charlie looked back, his eyes wide. He made a little coughing sound and swallowed. For a moment, nobody spoke.

Uncle Mike spoke first. 'Did what I *think* just happened, actually happen?'

'It happened. I saw it happen,' said Mum.

'In my whole life, I've never seen that happen,' said Dad.

'I certainly hope that never happens to me,' said Uncle Mike.

'What? What?' I almost yelled. 'What just happened? Tell me!'

I could barely hear Charlie as he whispered, 'I swallowed Dibby Doo.'

I suppose I should feel bad about it, but I don't. Charlie didn't mind. In fact he was proud. As he ate his ice cream he told everyone that Dibby Doo likes ice cream too. And he said that Dibby Doo was really lucky because now he could eat it and swim in it inside Charlie's tummy.

Mum wasn't so happy though. As she cleared up the plates, she did a little scream again: another woodlouse.

'That's Wobbly Woo!' shouted Charlie. 'I going to swallow him so he can play with Dibby Doo.'

He reached out to pick it up, but lightning Dad struck again: he swept Wobbly Woo into his hand, opened the window and threw him into the garden.

'Wobbly Woo needs to get home for his tea too,'

said Dad. 'And you need to get ready for bed.'

After lots of moaning, Charlie grabbed his Tic Tac box and was dragged off by Mum to brush his teeth and put on his dinosaur onesie. I stayed up because I'm older. I played Rock, Paper, Scissors with Uncle Mike, but he's a cheater because he invents new things like 'Steamroller' and 'Dynamite' which he says will beat anything.

Charlie came down for his bedtime kiss.

'Kissy kissy! Kissy kissy!' he shouted, running across the kitchen. 'Who wants sloppy, who wants licky, who wants normal?'

'Pucker up, little man, I like them sloppy,' said Uncle Mike, opening his arms for a cuddle. 'Hey, why the cross-eyes?'

Uncle Mike was right. Charlie looked even crazier than normal. His eyes were staring at the end of his nose and he had a naughty grin on his face.

If you've never tried it, staring at the end of your nose is *incredibly* hard. Try it now. It makes my tummy feel funny.

But for once, Charlie wasn't being weird. His eyes had locked onto something: a big red spot on the end of his nose. And as he got closer, the red spot had black spots on it.

When he reached me and Uncle Mike, there it was: a ladybird, sitting perfectly still on his schnozzle.

'I found my baby bird!' said Charlie.

'He's very comfy,' said Uncle Mike, 'but I think it's time your ladybird went home.' He reached out towards Charlie.

'No!' said Charlie, backing away.

But maybe the ladybird was smart because it opened its little round red wings and zipped off. Our heads did dizzy spiral patterns as we followed it in circles around the room. It flew through the window and off into the evening.

For the second time that day, nobody spoke.

'Bye bye baby bird,' said Charlie, eventually. His eyes were shining, and his voice wobbled. I touched his arm, and he pushed his bottom back between my legs. I put my arms around his warm tummy.

'Bye bye baby bird. See you on the next hug bunt.'

And he turned round, wrapped his arms around me and put his head on my chest.

The Animal Park

'You can take three things, no more,' said Mum from the kitchen. Charlie was sitting in the hall in front of a big pile of stuff. He wanted to take *everything* to the Animal Park.

Here's what I saw – and take a deep breath if you're reading this out loud. There was my old dolly buggy, a phone charger, a bottle of bubble mixture, several bananas, poster paints, a packet of pitta bread, a toilet roll, toy binoculars, a can of beer, a tube of glitter, a sock, a packet of tights and a box of make-up, Dad's work badge that he hangs round his neck, a sandcastle bucket, and a whistle. I may have forgotten some other stuff.

Dad appeared and did a giant step over Charlie and his goodies. 'Hey, what're you doing with these, soldier?' he said, pulling his work badge and the can of beer out of the pile.

'Daddy, that's *my* necklace,' complained Charlie, 'and the beer is for my tiger!'

'I don't think tigers drink beer,' said Dad.

'Yes. Dey. Do,' said Charlie, stamping his feet. 'And dey drink *all* the water in the tap. And dey eat *all* the sand witches. And dey eat all –'

'Ah,' said Dad. 'I know what you're saying. Still, if a tiger turns up for tea today, my little mucker, he'll have to go thirsty. I'm drinking this.'

Charlie stared at Dad with fierce x-ray eyes. Maybe he doesn't like being called a little mucker.

'Turn that frown upside down,' I said to Charlie as I waited by the stairs. Dad says that to me all the time, and it drives me crazy. Charlie tried to throw a banana at me. But as he swung his podgy arm back he let go, and the banana landed on his head.

'Naughty narna,' he said. 'You not coming wiv me now.'

After lots of swapping he decided he wanted to take the rest of the bananas (the good ones), paints and the toilet roll. One by one he shoved them into his ladybird rucksack.

If you've read the first stories I wrote about

Charlie, then you'll know that the last time Charlie was alone with felt tips he did something very naughty, and a builder got mega angry. This time he had paints, and BAD THINGS were going to happen. But I'm not the grown-up, so I didn't say anything.

And at least he would have a spare toilet roll in case he needed a poo.

The Animal Park is brilliant. It has ice creams, doughnuts, swings, a roundabout and giraffes. And in the shop they have millions of different coloured rubbers, and some of them smell of strawberries. I think I might want to work in a rubber shop when I grow up.

'What do you want to see most, kids?' asked Mum.

'The anteaters,' I said straight away. Have you ever seen an anteater? They're amazing! Their noses are like long bendy vacuum cleaner attachments, they have a wiry, wormy tongue and they're thin, as if they've been run over by a steamroller. I'm not joking: find pictures on

Google, it's like someone made them up.

'What about you, Charlie?' said Mum.

'The hellyfants. Nuffink else. And the tigers. Nuffink else. And the grillers. And the dina-sores. That's it, nuffink else,' said Charlie, and he charged off up the path.

'Good luck finding those dina-sores!' I shouted after him. What a silly billy.

I'd never known it so chocka-blocka. There were grannies and granddads, grown-ups with pushchairs and lots and lots of children. Not long after we'd started our visit we had to move out of the way for one of those beeping electric cars. In the back sat a boy a little older than Charlie.

Charlie stared hard. 'I want go in the car.'

'That's not how it works, Charlie boy,' said Dad. 'That lad's got a broken leg, it's in plaster.' The boy had a pair of crutches tucked up next to him on the seat.

'I want a broken leg,' said Charlie.

'That is the dumbest thing I've ever heard,' I said.

'Thank you Harry, that's unnecessary,' said Mum. 'Nobody *wants* a broken leg, Charlie, it just happens sometimes if you have a bad accident.

Come on, let's visit the lemurs.'

Ah yes, I forgot to tell you about lemurs. Do you know what they are? They're like monkeys, except that they're quite small and have long tails. And the best bit is that they have a cage that's so big you can walk right into it and around a path and get close to them.

When we got inside there were animal women talking about lemurs, and two of them were sitting on a post. (The lemurs were sitting on a post I mean, not the animal women, that would be weird.)

There were loads of people taking selfies and the animal women were feeding them fruit from a big bucket. (They were feeding the lemurs I mean, not the people taking selfies, that would also be weird.)

We tried to see but the grown-ups were blocking our view. Charlie got bored and toddled off.

'I'll meet you at the end,' I said to Mum.

'Sure,' she replied. 'Don't go out of the gate. And make sure you stick with Charlie!'

I zigzagged my way through the grown-ups' legs, ran up the path and around the first corner. No sign of Charlie. Round another corner and still no Charlie, but instead – in front of me on the path – sat another lemur, chewing on a piece of apple.

I did crab-steps along the path so I could get past and still keep an eye on the lemur, just in case. By this time the path was deserted although animals were rustling up in the trees, and I'm certain they were watching me with their big round eyes.

Another bend. On the path, a chunk of apple. And another. In fact I was now following a line of apple chunks which led off into the trees.

By now I was a bit scared. It felt like I'd swallowed a bag of caterpillars. But my head was smarter than my tummy because it was thinking, 'I wonder where that apple trail goes?'

And so I told my tummy to behave and I stepped off the path. Around the next tree another lemur was sitting, chewing away. But the trail continued, so I tiptoed around him and followed the line of apple pieces around a big rock.

'SHHHH!' said someone nearby.

This gave me such a surprise I almost wet myself. Charlie appeared by my side, crouching.

'Get down!' he whispered. 'We be very quiet.'

I opened my mouth to ask him what was going on, but he pointed. There, on the edge of a small patch of grass, a mummy lemur sat with her baby. The fruit trail ended here; the apple pieces led right up to Charlie's ladybird rucksack.

It was lying on its side. Somehow he'd used sticks to hold it open. And inside were three bright yellow bananas.

As we stayed hidden the baby lemur walked forward and sat at the entrance to the rucksack, with his head on one side. He put out his paw and touched the zip. Then, with one small jump, he was inside the rucksack!

'NOW!' shouted Charlie, and he ran towards it.

'Stop it Charlie that's NAUGHTY!' I yelled, but I wasn't the only one who had something to say. The mummy lemur shot forward, making a screechy, howly sound. Charlie screamed back, showing his pointy little teeth like an animal. He grabbed his rucksack but the baby lemur clambered out onto Charlie's shoulders. And with a huge leap he grabbed hold of his mummy, climbed onto her back and they were both gone, streaking up a tree.

Charlie plopped down onto his bottom. His

whole body shook, and there were tears in his eyes. I wanted to cuddle him.

'But I want a leemer for my treasure box at pee-school,' he said. 'Is not fair.'

'Life's not fair,' I said. I pulled him up, grabbed his rucksack, and we walked back to the path.

(It's true that, about life not being fair. Last week I got seven out of ten in our maths quiz and my best friend Iona did too, but she got a merit sticker and I didn't. Iona said we should share it but when she took it off, it didn't have any sticky left and it fell on the floor.)

As we reached the path Charlie disappeared behind a tree and came out clutching his toilet rolls and paints, which he shoved into his bag.

'What's the toilet roll for, Charlie?' I asked.

'Is for your poo-poo head,' said Charlie, grinning. He had already forgotten about his lemur plan.

'Oi!' I shouted. 'Don't be cheeky!'

Too late: Charlie had already run round the next bend, his arms waggling and his fat nappy-bottom wiggling.

I caught up with him at the gates. He stood, good as gold, holding Mum's hand.

'Where you been Harry?' he asked.

My mouth fell open. He is unbelievable.

'Yes, where have you been, Harry?' asked Dad. 'And what's all this I hear about you trying to cuddle a lemur?'

'What?' I said. 'Me? Are you joking? I didn't do anything! It was Charlie, he tried to put one in his bag! I was –'

'OK, OK, Harry, keep your wig on. I believe you,' said Dad. 'And that's more than I can say for this cheeky monkey,' he said. And he ruffled Charlie's hair.

The next bit of the Animal Park is my favourite: it's a long, long path with all the best animals on it, and some other ones. You begin with tigers, then lions, then other big cats and dogs. After that come the monkeys: the little ones first, getting bigger and bigger until the last cage where the baboons live.

So we started with the tigers. Sometimes they walk right next to the fence, rubbing themselves against it and looking at you a bit oddly, like they fancy a snack. The kind of snack that has two arms, two legs, curly ginger hair and a stinky brother.

But today the tigers were sleeping in the sun. It took a while to spot them because they were so still except for their tummies rising and falling. Occasionally their tails would twitch and waft around, perhaps when they were having a funny tiger dream about knocking on someone's door and being invited in for tea and beer.

We stood for a minute, eating flapjacks.

'Wakey wakey tigers!' shouted Charlie. 'You need a wee wee? You want my fatjack?' And you'll hardly believe this, because he threw part of his snack into the tigers' enclosure!

'Charlie!' said Mum, grabbing him. 'That is *very* naughty. Tigers do *not* eat flapjack.'

'They prefer eating chubby three-year-olds,' said Dad. 'Especially cheeky boys.'

The nearest tiger pushed himself to his feet, padded over to the fence and lowered his head. With his eyes fixed on Dad his huge tongue came out and he hooked the chunk of flapjack into his mouth. The tiger raised his head and stood like a statue, staring at Dad.

'Whoa!' said Dad to the tiger. 'Back off, big boy.

It was only my little joke.' But as he said this Dad's feet did a shuffle, and he moved a bit further away.

'Daddy scared,' said Charlie, still chewing. 'Hey pussy cat, you want more fatjack?'

But as he reached out to throw another chunk, Mum yanked on the hood of his jacket and pulled him away. 'Time to move on,' she said.

'Grr,' said the tiger, baring its teeth.

'Right back at you, buddy,' said Dad, sticking his tongue out at the tiger.

I think we know who Charlie gets his naughty ideas from, don't we?

A bit later we all stood still, looking into the cage of the African hunting dogs.

'There's nothing in there,' I said. 'Let's go.'

'Hang on,' said Mum. 'They're pretty well camouflaged. Keep searching.'

'Mummy?' said Charlie. 'What's camo, camo, camo, camo, camo –'

'Quick, Charlie's stuck again,' said Dad. 'Someone turn him off and on again.'

'Don't be mean, Tom,' said Mum. 'Camouflage

is when an animal disguises itself so it can't be spotted.'

'Like when I wear my princess outfit?' said Charlie.

'Erm, something like that,' said Mum. 'Hey, there's one moving!'

Bingo! I spotted one. In fact if I stared hard I could spot browny-grey dogs all over the place. But they were the same colour as the bushes so only people with super laser eyes like mine would spot them all.

'I can see them now,' I said. 'But they're only dogs. My best friend Gabby has a dog, and it's much bigger than that.'

'Yes, but I bet Gabby's dog can't run as fast as a car,' said Dad, reading the information board.

'I bet she can,' I said. 'She's called Mrs Whippy.'

'OK then,' said Dad. 'Does she make herself sick, and give the sick to her puppies to eat?'

'Bleurrgh,' I said. 'That's disgusting. Mrs Whippy wouldn't do that.'

'And would she kill other puppies to make sure there's enough food for her own babies? These bad boys would,' said Dad, pointing at the African dogs.

'Tom!' said Mum.

'That's mean!' I said.

'What?' said Dad. 'It's true! Harry and I are having a serious nature chat. Although I admit it's turning into a game of Doggy Top Trumps.'

'Mrs Whippy does lots of trumps,' I said. 'They smell of cabbage.'

'That reminds me of someone else I know, eh Charlie?' said Dad. 'Charlie? Where is the little trumpet?'

Dad scratched his head. 'He was definitely here a moment ago.'

Well Charlie certainly wasn't here any more. In fact, there weren't that many people around at all now. We squinted back down the path: nothing, just another of those buggies in the distance.

'Maybe he's been munched by a tiger,' I said.

'Not funny,' said Mum. 'Tom, we need to keep a better eye on him. This is ridiculous. You need to go back and find him, pronto.'

'But he was right here!' Dad said. 'He must have gone ahead.'

'He didn't,' I said, 'he's just there.' Can you guess where? If you guessed the buggy, you were right. His grinning face peered out at us, next to one of the animal men.

'Mummeeee!' he shouted as the buggy pulled to a stop. 'The man animal gived me a lift.'

'So I see,' said Mum, raising one eyebrow. 'Say thank you, Charlie.'

'Fank you, Mr man animal.'

'You're welcome, sunshine,' said the man, who didn't mind that Charlie had called him an animal. 'And I hope that leg gets better soon.'

'What leg?' I said, but I didn't need to ask because Charlie had stepped down from the buggy and was now dragging his leg along the ground like an incredibly heavy sausage.

'And stay away from that sister of yours, she sounds like trouble!' shouted the animal man with a grin as he drove off.

'What did he mean by that?' I said. 'What has Charlie been saying?'

By now Charlie had dragged himself up to Mum and was standing close, looking very guilty.

'Ow,' said Charlie, in a matter-of-fact voice.

'What's going on here, Charlie? What on earth

did you tell that man? And why are you limping like that?'

'My leg is boken,' said Charlie quietly.

'Hmm. And how did you get this broken leg, dare I ask?'

'Harry hit me and broked it,' muttered Charlie.

'WHAT?' I said.

'She hit me wiv a flying pan.'

'He's mad!' I said.

'She did it when I was asleep,' Charlie whispered.

'Dad! Mum!' I was hardly able to speak. 'He's making it all up! I –'

'OK, Harry, relax,' said Dad. 'I'm pretty certain Charlie's leg will get better quickly. Luckily I've brought some magic tablets.' He pulled a packet of Mini Cheddars out of his coat pocket. 'You sound like you need a snack, little munchkin.'

'Cheeses!' shouted Charlie, running straight across to Dad.

In one smooth motion Dad slipped the Mini Cheddars back into his pocket, whisked Charlie up into the air and dangled him upside down.

'It's a miracle!' shouted Dad. 'Call the newspapers, this boy is cured!'

I'd had enough of this. I ran ahead to be on my own, without any annoying, noisy, fibbing, spoiled, smelly, dirty little brothers.

I couldn't wait to visit the baboons again. The last time we came, two of them started screeching and throwing poo at each other. Seriously, they did poos out of their bright red bottoms into their hands, and threw the lumps right across the cage!

Mum told me that I once ate my own poo when I was a baby. Have you ever eaten yours? I don't remember what it tasted like, do you? It's a bit lumpy, I expect, and I'm sure it doesn't taste of chocolate. I wouldn't like it if someone threw a poo at me.

Anyway, I was hoping the baboons would throw poo again, but unfortunately they were all playing nicely this time. Mum, Dad and Charlie walked up to join me.

'So Harry,' said Dad. 'Which one is your new boyfriend? Is it the one with the red bottom?'

'They've all got red bottoms,' I said, 'and you're not funny.'

'Ah, my mistake,' said Dad. 'But I'm sure Charlie can find himself a nice monkey-girlfriend. What about that little one at the back? No? Or how about this big fella near the front?'

'They need botty cream,' said Charlie.

'They're supposed to be like that, aren't they Mum?' I said. 'They like showing off.'

'True, Charlie, though it's only the girls who have the red bottoms,' said Mum. 'They think that boy baboons like them.'

'*I* like dem,' said Charlie, 'dey are funny.' He rummaged in his rucksack and pulled out his toilet roll. Very carefully, he started to tear off sheets and stuff each one into a hole in the fence.

'Are you going to let him do that?' I asked Mum and Dad.

'Who's turn is it this time?' sighed Mum, leaning on Dad's shoulder.

'Dis one is for you, dis one is for you, dis one is for you,' said Charlie, pointing at each of the baboons. 'Don't use too much, is a waste. And wash your poo-poo monkey hands.'

He got to the end of the row. 'There, finished. Now dey can wipe their bottoms,' he said. 'Can I haf a red bottom Daddy?'

'If you had a red bottom like that, I'd take you straight to the doctor,' said Dad, pulling the pieces of toilet roll out of the fence. 'Or maybe lend you to Santa in case Rudolph is off sick. Come on, let's get an ice cream.'

The rest of the day turned out brilliantly, like it always does. We had ice cream and doughnuts and we saw right inside a hippo's mouth. Charlie fell off the swing. He cried for a bit and ran away and we lost him for ages, but that's normal.

'What a great day,' said Dad as we walked back to the car. 'Nobody got eaten, we didn't get thrown out, and we found a hairy girlfriend for Harry.' I smacked him on the bottom.

'I'll settle for that,' said Mum. 'In you get, little man,' and she opened the door for Charlie.

Charlie stepped up into the car. 'Hang on,' said Mum, 'what have you done, Charlie?'

She lifted him out and looked down his trousers. 'Quick, Tom! I think he hurt himself when he fell off the swing! There's blood everywhere!'

'Seriously?' said Dad, who dropped the change bag and ran round.

'Help!' shouted Mum, pulling off his trousers. 'We need a doctor!'

'Hold on love, are you sure it's that bad?' said Dad, who couldn't see very well from behind Mum.

'Yes, I am,' she said. 'He must have ruptured something, it's filled his nappy.'

Charlie said nothing.

There were people all around us, getting into their cars ready to go home. A woman in a shiny green sari came running over from the nearest car.

'Can I help?' she asked. 'I'm a doctor.'

'It's my son,' said Mum. 'He fell off a swing and I think he's cut himself quite badly. There's blood everywhere.'

The lady kneeled down in front of Charlie. 'Hey there little one, what's your name?'

'Charlie,' he said. 'I'm free.'

'Excellent. Let's take a little look, shall we?' And the lady gently tore off Charlie's nappy pants.

I screamed. Mum screamed. Two children in the car next door screamed. His bottom shone bright red, with blood dripping onto the floor.

The lady peered and then bent a bit closer. She put her finger in the blood and sniffed it, which I thought was a strange thing to do. Shouldn't she be calling an ambulance?

'I don't think there's too much to worry about here,' she said to Mum. 'Although you might find something missing from your art cupboard when you get home.' She wiped her finger on the grass and ruffled Charlie's hair. 'You've got a funny one here and no mistake.'

I hadn't got a clue what she meant. Neither did Mum. 'I'm sorry, what are you saying?' she said, a bit rudely.

I moved to get a better view and stepped on Charlie's ladybird rucksack. It squashed right down under my foot. Bing! Suddenly, I knew *everything*.

'Mum, I know what's happened,' I said. 'That's not blood. It's Charlie's red paint.'

Mum sat down, put her elbows on her knees and gazed at the sky. 'Give me strength,' she said, before turning to the lady. 'Thank you so much.'

Dad started to chuckle. The doctor lady smiled. 'I think I'm done here. Have a lovely trip home,' she said as she walked away.

'I told you he'd need to see a doctor,' laughed Dad. Charlie started to climb into the car. 'Hold your horses, tootsie pants!' he said, grabbing Charlie. 'You're not going anywhere near my car seats with a bum like that!'

Eventually Mum turned to Charlie. 'Are you trying to give me a heart attack?' she said. 'Bring me the wet wipes, Charlie.'

'I not Charlie I is a baboon,' said Charlie. And do you know what he did? He bent over and pointed his big red bottom at the children in the other cars. After the shock of having a bottom pointed at them they started pointing and laughing.

The dad leaned out of the window. 'Rather you than me,' he said, as they drove away. 'You could stop traffic with that thing!'

Charlie looked pleased with himself. 'And now I do a poo and frow it,' he said, and he put his hands on his bottom.

'NO CHARLIE!!!' shouted Mum, Dad and me together.

'Only joking,' sang Charlie, with a big smile. And he lay down on his back with his big red painty bum in the air and waited for someone to clean him up.

Puppy

Have you ever kissed a dog? I have. Well actually I didn't have a choice because Mrs Whippy, my best friend Gabby's dog, kissed me. She jumped up, put her paws on my tummy, and licked me all over my face with her hot wet doggy tongue and flappy red lips. It smelled of dog food, obviously, but also compost and toilets. It was like being kissed by the bin. Yuckety-yuck.

So do you have a dog? Does it poo on the pavement? Lots of dogs do that in our town, especially on the path by the church that goes to school. Their owners should put the poo into those poo bags and take it home, but they never do.

When I was little I used to sit on the front of the buggy, between Charlie's legs, and be Mummy's Official Poo Spotter. Whenever one came up, I'd shout and point. 'It's a big brown one!' or 'It's a lumpy one!' or 'It's a sloppy one!'

Mum would do a zigzag around it to make sure she didn't get any on the buggy wheels. Once I didn't notice a big brown one because I was too busy crunching Hula Hoops. Mum went right through it, squish-squash. We had to leave the buggy outside in the rain for a week because it smelled so horrid and Mum and Dad couldn't decide who should clean it because they both said they were unusually busy that week.

But even though dogs give you stinky kisses and poo on the pavement, I wish we had a dog. They're cute. I've asked Dad a million times, but he says our house is too small and he likes his shut-eye too much.

'Have I got a shut-eye?' Charlie had asked, scrunching up his face.

'Daddy means he likes sleeping,' said Mum. 'Daddy is a lazy lump who doesn't like getting up early.'

'Ah, if only I was as perfect as you, Little Miss Rise and Shine,' said Dad.

Mum smiled and flicked her hair back, pretending to be in a shampoo advert.

'But I still reckon I'd be the one walking the dog around the block in my pyjamas,' said Dad, 'and that's why it's never going to happen.'

'You're a meanie,' I said.

'A meany-beany,' said Mum.

'A meany-beany bing bong,' said Charlie.

Dad smiled, shrugged his shoulders, and carried on washing up.

But a few weeks ago Mum told us that her friend Carla was going on holiday and asked if Charlie and I would like to care for her dog.

'Yes!' I shouted. 'What type of dog is it?'

'A hot dog!' shouted Charlie.

'Not a hot dog,' said Mum. 'In fact it's not a dog, it's a puppy. And that's why Carla wants to leave him with a family like ours. He's too young to be left in kennels. She'll bring him round tomorrow.'

And so that's what happened. The doorbell rang and I jumped off the sofa with Charlie right behind me. But as I was about to open the door a dog started barking on the other side. I don't like barking, do you? It's scary. So we waited for Mum to come, and stood behind her, just in case.

'Hey Carla, come on in,' said Mum.

'Hey Liz. Hello everyone,' said Mum's friend Carla. 'Come and meet Tuppence. Don't be afraid, he wouldn't hurt a fly.'

It wasn't the flies that bothered me. They have enough trouble with Charlie. Dad once told him that if you leave a raisin on the kitchen table it grows wings and turns into a fly. Ever since then he's tried to grab them out of the air and eat them.

Mum pushed us forward; Carla was holding the dog tightly by the collar.

'Mummy, you said Tuppence was a puppy,' I said.

'He *is* a puppy, Harry,' said Mum. 'But... well he's grown since I saw him last, hasn't he?'

'He's massive!' I said.

This dog was as tall as Charlie, except with more teeth. His hair was the same sandy colour as mine, except much shorter, and his eyes were brown like mine, except much bigger. His paws were doing a little dance on the wooden floor, making a tippity-tap noise, and he was breathing noisily – 'hurr, hurr, hurr' – like he'd come last in a cross-country race.

'He's very excited to meet you,' said Carla, pulling Tuppence into the living room.

'I is scared,' said Charlie, who had disappeared back behind Mum.

'It'll be fine,' said Mum. We sat down and straight away Tuppence jumped up onto the sofa with us, climbing all over our laps and turning round and round.

'Tuppence, get down!' said Carla, but it didn't sound like she meant it, and Tuppence thought so too because he didn't get down.

'I do let him sit on the sofa at home, but of course you don't have to do that.'

Mum didn't say anything.

Tuppence flopped onto his belly, lying right across my lap with his head on Charlie's leg. Charlie had both hands up in the air, terrified. Tuppence was delighted, however, and his tail thumped down on Mum's arm. His tummy felt warm, and I stroked his back.

'Ugh, doggy done dwibble on my towsers,' said Charlie.

We laughed. 'Never mind Charlie, he does that sometimes, but only on the people he likes,' said Carla.

'But *I* not like it,' wailed Charlie.

'Don't be a baby,' I said, 'it will wash off.' Tuppence's warm tummy felt lovely on my lap. I stroked him again. 'I like Tuppence.'

'Thank you so much,' said Carla. 'I couldn't bear to think of leaving him with strangers. I'm sure he won't be any trouble, he's a little darling.'

Tuppence's tummy felt warmer than ever.

'I'm sure we'll be fine,' said Mum. 'Now is there anything else to tell us?'

The warm feeling on my lap spread out, down the sides of my thighs. That was weird.

'No, you're all set,' said Carla. 'As long as he gets his walk first thing and plenty of runabouts, he'll be good as gold.'

The warmness had now reached my bottom. In fact, it felt a bit like I'd wet myself. Actually, thinking about it…

'Yuck! Mummy, Tuppence has done a wee!'

'What?' said Mum.

'Oh Tuppence!' said Carla, grabbing his collar and pulling him off our laps. My light blue trousers were now dark blue.

'I'm so sorry Harry, he does that sometimes,' said Carla.

'But let me guess,' said Mum, 'only on the people he likes?'

'Ah, umm, yes, I suppose so,' said Carla. I jumped up and pulled my trousers straight off. I didn't care if people saw my pants, I didn't want doggy wee on my leg.

This was basically like Christmas to Charlie, of course. He laughed, and pointed. 'Harry done a wee-wee! Harry done a wee-wee!'

'Aargh!' I yelled. 'That's revolting!'

'I'm sorry, Harry,' said Carla, 'he's a bit excited. He won't –'

But I didn't hear any more because I was running upstairs to wash my dog-wee leg.

'A little darling.' That's what Carla had called Tuppence, but I wasn't so sure. Before Dad got home from work Tuppence had:

- Knocked a cup of juice on the floor with his tail (Mum shouted)
- Barked for, like, twenty minutes without stopping (I put my hands over my ears)
- Pushed Charlie over (Charlie cried)

- Weed on the carpet (Mum shouted again)
- Chased his tail (we laughed, and even Mum smiled a bit)
- Chewed Charlie's recorder (Charlie cried again)
- Chewed my jumper (Mum looked like she was going to cry)

And then, as if following secret orders, Tuppence climbed into his big red basket and fell fast asleep.

The front door opened.

'Daddy!' we shouted and ran to give him a hug. Well, not Mum – she stayed in the lounge, cleaning up the wee on the carpet.

'Hey my little bunch of parsnips, how are you?' said Dad. 'And how's our four-legged guest?'

'We got a doggy and he is *really* naughty!' said Charlie. 'He did the toilet on Harry's legs.'

'That sounds a trifle unwelcome,' said Dad, looking at Tuppence with soppy eyes. 'But he's a good-looking mutt, I must say.'

'It's true, Daddy,' I said. 'It was disgusting.'

'And he staying wiv us for two weeks!' said Charlie.

'I think it's fair to say that looking after

Tuppence was the worst idea we've ever had,' said Mum, sponge in hand. 'Tom, find me the Chinese takeaway menu and a bottle of wine.' And she went back to scrubbing the carpet.

Taking Tuppence to school made everything OK again. He dragged me up the hill for starters, and all my friends wanted to stroke him in the playground and ask me questions.

'When will he die?' asked Axel, straight away. I once overheard Mum tell Dad that Axel is a very funny boy, but he doesn't make me laugh.

'Ages,' I say.

'Never,' said Charlie firmly. He opened his eyes and mouth wide and stuck his chin out at Axel. He looked a bit weird, but that's because he was trying to do a Paddington hard stare.

'He's so cute! What's his name?' asked my best friend Charlotte.

'Tuppence. Daddy says he's a crossbreed.'

Tuppence wagged his tail.

'He not cross, he happy,' says Charlie.

'That means he's half one type of dog, half

another,' I said.

Charlie laughed at me and twirled round and round with his hands in the air. 'Arf an arf? Eh? Eh? Arf an arf? What you talkin' about Harry?' (He's learned to say that from Dad and it's so annoying.)

'It's a bit like you, Charlie.' Mum grabbed him by the wrists and stopped him spinning, because otherwise he gets dizzy and falls over. 'In a way, you're half Mummy, and half Daddy.'

'And a bit of doggy poo too,' I whispered to Charlotte, and we did our secret laugh. Mum pushed her lips out and frowned, which she does when she wants me to stop something.

Charlie paused, looking down at his body. 'This bit is Daddy,' he said, reaching down and patting his feet, 'coz Daddy runs faster.'

'Steady on there, Charlie,' said Mum, 'I don't cheat in races like Daddy.'

'I fink my knees are from Daddy too coz he's more knobbly than Mummy.'

'That's true,' said Mum. 'So which bits are from me, or am I going to regret this?'

'My bum-bum,' said Charlie, grabbing his bottom. 'And my boobies.' He planted his hands on his hips and started walking around the playground like a model.

'Oh lordy, Charlie!' said Mum, smiling. By now all my friends were screaming and shouting, laughing and pointing. A few of the mummies were joining in, too. Mum ran after Charlie to catch him and Charlotte and I ran after Mum, and Tuppence danced around in circles, wagging his tail.

Mr Jones the grumpy caretaker walked across and told Mum that dogs weren't allowed in the playground, and that she'd have to tie Tuppence to the railings outside.

How rude! As Mr Jones walked away, I hoped that Mr Jones would fall in a puddle right up to his middle, but unfortunately he didn't.

So next morning Mum tied up Tuppence, even though he made a sad, whiny sound. And I have to tell you that after we started doing that and I couldn't show him off to my friends, the fun stopped. Dad took him for a walk in the morning, Mum gave him his stinky dog food, and Charlie tickled his tummy. That wasn't fair because it meant I didn't have a doggy job to do.

Charlie became Tuppence's best friend, and Charlie loved it. Up and down the hall they trotted, and out into the garden. Sometimes Tuppence went first with Charlie trying to grab his tail. Sometimes Charlie led, often on his hands and knees like a dog, with Tuppence sniffing his bottom.

'Why does Tuppence smell my bottom?' Charlie asked.

'A good question,' said Mum. 'Doggies love bottoms. I'm not sure why. Does anyone know?' she asked her mummy friends who had come round to stand in the kitchen and drink tea.

'It's how they make friends,' said Jane.

'Bleurgh,' I said as I tried to find something to eat in the cupboard.

'Maybe doggies like the smell,' said Serena.

'That's weird.' I wrinkled my nose.

Charlie loved this idea, of course. He crawled up to me and tried to sniff my bottom, but I sat down and that stopped him. So he crawled round behind Jane. Just as she was drinking a slurp of tea, he pushed his nose right in and did a big sniff.

Jane made a weird noise. The kind of squawk a chicken would make if it fell over into a pond. It's hard to spell, but I'll try. To get this word to sound right, say it in a chicken voice.

'Wwwwwrrrarrrrk-ppppt-sssh!'

I'd never heard anyone make that sound before. Neither had Mum nor her friend Serena because they started laughing uncontrollably. But Serena had tea in her mouth too and because she was laughing, she couldn't swallow it. Her cheeks puffed out like two brown balloons, tears started dribbling down her face and tea started dribbling out of her nose! And the more she cried, the more Mum and Jane laughed.

It was too much for Serena. All the tea splurted out like a hosepipe that's popped off the tap, spraying all over her jumper and the floor. She bent right over, holding her tummy. 'Stop it everyone, I'm in agony here!'

Charlie looked up at Jane. 'Your bottom smells of conkers,' he said.

Serena, still doubled over, made a groaning noise. Charlie crawled over to her.

'You want me sniff *your* bottom?' he asked.

Serena pushed her face into her knees and started howling. Proper like-a-wolf howling. It was hard to tell if she was crying or laughing.

'Charlie,' said Mum, wiping her eyes, 'pack it in, I can't take it any more.'

'OK,' said Charlie. 'Come on Tuppence.' Tuppence wagged his tail and trotted out of the kitchen. Charlie, still on all fours, followed him out, waggling his bottom as he left.

So all that stuff I've been telling you about Tuppence happened in the first week. By the weekend Mum was hardly ever shouting or crying because Tuppence wasn't doing wees on the kitchen floor. Dad took him for walks in the mornings, although not in his pyjamas. And I had found out that if you rested your feet on Tuppence while you ate your dinner he would keep your toes nice and toasty.

Charlie still wouldn't leave Tuppence alone. He put his princess dress over Tuppence's head 'to make him look pretty', but Tuppence didn't want to look pretty and crawled out.

He tried to get Tuppence's tangles untangled. Tuppence didn't like that either, and I laughed until I realised he was using my hairbrush.

He even tried to get rid of Tuppence's stinky breath. He put a massive worm of toothpaste on Mum's electric toothbrush and stuck it in Tuppence's mouth. Tuppence definitely *did* like that: he kept licking the toothbrush and trying to chew on it as it went grrrr-brrrr inside his mouth. Loads of white dribble came foaming out, and glooped all over the carpet. And I mean loads. Naughty boys once put washing up liquid in our town fountain, and it looked a bit like that. I reckon there was enough to fill a bucket or two.

But Mum wasn't so amazed, in fact she screamed. Really loud. And blamed me for not telling her. How unfair.

'Right, I don't care how gloomy it is outside, we are going to the park,' she said after she'd calmed down and ordered a new toothbrush on the internet. 'Get your shoes and coats on, we're off.'

'Have a lovely time, my darling family,' said Dad. He made himself a bit more comfy on the sofa and swiped his phone.

'No chance,' said Mum, 'you're coming too. Grab your coat, mister.'

Dad did a big sigh. That was a bit rich, as Granny says, because he was only looking at Facebook, I saw it on his screen.

Tuppence didn't understand much. If you said something like 'Don't wee on the carpet,' or 'Move over, I can't see the telly,' all he heard was 'burble burble burble,' so he took no notice.

But he had a secret doggy code word: 'Park'. As soon as Mum said that he jumped out of his basket like he had been stung by a bee and rushed up and down the hall, barking and rubbing his bottom on people. Dad grabbed him, slid his collar on and attached his lead.

'It's going to be dark in half an hour,' said Dad, opening the front door. 'Either that or the end of the world is coming.'

The cars had their lights on, and all the neighbours were shutting their curtains so you couldn't tell that they were secretly watching *The X Factor*. In fact it reminded me of that bit at the end of *The Tiger Who Came to Tea*. Have you read that book? It's not for big children like us, but I used to read it when I was little. They all go out at the end because the tiger has scoffed all their food, and it's dark, and the shop lights are on. Except that they were going out for chips, and we were going out for a walk in the cold with a crazy dog.

But we left because once Mum says something's

going to happen, it happens. (I learned that lesson ages ago when she said she would throw my dinner in the bin if I didn't stop singing at the table. I didn't stop, so she did it: all my beans, sausages, everything. I started crying, and Charlie told Mum off because he said she should recycle everything because thcy say so at preschool, and Mum said that's true but you can't recycle baked beans into anything, and Charlie said oh yes you can, and she said OK what then mister smarty pants, and Charlie said you can put the beans into a cushion to make it more comfy, and we all started laughing again. I still didn't get any dinner though.)

What was I talking about? Oh yes, we were off to the park. What is your park like? Is it one of the good ones with swings and a zip wire and roundabouts? Or is it a boring one with trees and grass and maybe a lake? I hope you have a good one. I don't want to show off, but we have both: a good one up the hill, and a boring one down at the bottom.

'I want go to the uvver one,' said Charlie as we started walking down the hill.

'It's too late for the swings, Master Scroggins,' said Dad. (If you find out who Master Scroggins is, will you let me know? It's another of Dad's silly names.)

Tuppence stopped to sniff a car wheel, which he does just before he has a wee. Dad yanked his collar. 'Come on you disgraceful hound, we haven't got time for that. Mum wants to frogmarch us around the park to make us better people, so that's what we shall do.'

'March like froggies!' Charlie crouched down on the pavement and puffed his cheeks out. 'Ribbit, ribbit, ribbit, ribbit, ribbit, ribbit… '

'I'm losing the will to live already,' said Dad. 'Let's get that froggy bottom of yours to the park.'

Charlie jumped up. 'I want to drive Tuppence!' he said in a shouty voice he uses when he's trying to argue with nobody.

'Charlie!' I said. 'You don't drive a dog. And stop shouting, you're making my ears hurt.'

'I'm with you there, sister,' said Dad. (I'm not his sister, in case you're wondering.) 'What should I give you to stop you shouting for the rest of the day?'

'A million and a half pounds?' said Charlie.

Dad laughed. 'That's a bit more than I was thinking. How about 10p, and I'll give it to you when you're 18 years old?' Dad held out his hand to Charlie.

Charlie tilted his head and did his thinking face. 'Deal.' He shook Dad's hand. He's always doing deals with Dad.

'Special offer: you get a free dog with every handshakc,' said Dad, and gave Charlie the lead.

So Charlie took it and trotted after Tuppence, giggling. I pushed my hand into Dad's pocket, which is always nice and warm. Sometimes it has sweets in it, but not this time.

'I'll be sad when Tuppence goes back, will you Daddy?'

'Hmm.'

We walked on for a bit. Thump.

'Waaaaahh! Arrumm-grrrr! Mummeeee!'

That, in case you can't work it out, was the sound of Charlie falling over on the pavement, and crying. Have you ever tried to spell the sound of someone crying? It's impossible. You try.

Anyway, I bet you know what it sounds like in your head, and that's the noise he made. Tuppence had pulled too hard on the lead and dragged Charlie over. Now he was snuffling around him as if he was trying to say doggy sorry.

Dad picked Charlie up and gave Tuppence's lead to me instead as we walked through the park gates.

'Just a quick loop through the woods and back home for tea,' said Mum, who had been walking ahead on her own. 'Blast away those Sunday cobwebs.'

She looked at Charlie with his mouth hanging open. He was about to say something silly about cobwebs. 'And no, there are no giant spiders in the park today. Or sharks,' she added.

'Oh,' said Charlie. He ran ahead, chased by a yapping Tuppence with me running behind, holding onto the lead tightly.

We were following the footpath along the edge of the woods now. It's a windy, twisty route that can't make its mind up. Sometimes you think it's going to go straight into the playing fields to play football but it does a big loop and shoots back into the trees to play there instead.

There are lots of little paths that turn off this one into the wood, too. Some shortcuts chop off the corners, others zoom away to dark places. Once, Charlie, Dad and I went exploring down one of these paths. We walked for ages; past blown-down trees with spaces inside to hide and eat crisps, across a slippery bridge, around a spooky stone cottage that Dad said was definitely haunted, and out to fields on the other side. But the fields had massive cows in them, and Dad is scared of cows so we had to come home.

Back on our cobwebs walk, Charlie, Tuppence and I ran and ran, until we were way ahead of Mum and Dad. Charlie's yellow welly boots made him easy to spot, which was a good job because you couldn't tell where you were going, especially in the gloomy bits under the trees.

He turned off the main path onto one of the little shortcuts. 'We go boo to Mummy!' he shouted. Tuppence barked back to show he was listening, and we followed Charlie further into the wood.

Out of the corner of my eye something moved in the leaves by the side of the path. Tuppence stopped so suddenly I had to jump right over him. I reckon I would have won a prize at school sports day with this jump. But I forgot about Tuppence's lead. I tripped right over it and landed right on my bottom.

'Tuppence!' I shouted as he ran into the leaves, barking like crazy. Or at least he tried to run, but he pulled the tangle tighter and tighter around my legs. It was like the start of a rubbish magic trick.

Tuppence took no notice of me and my shouting. The leaves rustled: a squirrel. It boinged up off the ground, whizzed along a fallen log, and did a massive zoomy jump right over Tuppence's head onto the trunk of a tree. Seriously, this must have been a superhero squirrel, or a squirrel with wings.

This rocket jump sent Tuppence completely nutty. He pogoed up and down. But the short lead had tangled around me so my legs bounced up and down every time he did a jump. Ouch-ouch-ouch-ouch. He barked so much the barks almost joined together into one big bark.

'Tuppence!' I shouted. 'I'm stuck and you're sticking me!'

I rolled over to see if I could untangle myself that way but I made it worse and brought Tuppence's dribbly yapping face even closer to mine. I tried to unclip his lead, but he kept flapping his tongue all over the place like a soggy pink dishcloth and I did *not* want another doggy kiss. I wriggled and squirmed and managed to push the lead down my legs and over my ankles.

But just as I did that, Tuppence gave another tug, and the lead pulled my trainer right off. Ping! Well it didn't actually make that noise, but it did fly off, like a bogey when you flick it. (I never do that but I caught Dad doing it once, out of the car window.)

So now I'd got the lead sorted but I only had one shoe. So I got up onto one foot, wobbling like crazy as Tuppence tried to pull me over again, and I hopped off the path and over towards my trainer.

That's what I was doing when Mum and Dad came round the corner, holding hands (yuck).

'So there you are. What flavour of crazy are you up to now, Harry?' said Dad. 'Have you lost your wooden leg?'

'Well I was, y'know, well Tuppence saw a squirrel, and I fell over, and... '

'You'll be wanting this then, little Miss,' said Mum, holding up my trainer which she'd fetched from a pile of leaves. 'Tuppence, zip it, for goodness sake!'

'What's it worth, Harry? Tidy your bedroom? Do your homework without moaning?' Mum held the trainer high above my head, teasing me.

'Mummy! Mummy! Mummeeee!' I hopped as high as I could, which wasn't that high. It's quite difficult.

'How about... you wipe Charlie's bottom for the next week. Yes, that should do it. Here you go.' She dropped the trainer.

By now the squirrel had vanished up into the tree, and Tuppence lost interest. At last.

'Anyway, what've you done with Charlie, Harry? He's usually in the middle of this kind of nonsense,' said Mum.

'Err, I don't know.' I tried to get my fingernail into the knot of my shoelace. I hate that.

'Harry, What do you mean? He was with you. You were with him. You were together.'

'Well I *was* with him, but he ran ahead and the super-squirrel appeared.'

'A super-squirrel?' said Dad. 'What, do you mean like a –'

Mum interrupted. 'Where. Is. Charlie.' But she wasn't asking a question. She said the words like she wanted to fire them into my brain, although her eyes were darting everywhere.

'I DON'T KNOW!' I shouted back. My face began to burn. It wasn't my fault. Why did Mum have to be so rude?

'He won't be far away,' said Dad. 'CHARLIE! CHARLEEEEEE!' When Dad shouts, it's loud.

I joined in. 'Charlie! Charlie! Charlie!' Normally I get told off for shouting, do you? But now I could shout as loud as I liked. Tuppence thought this was a great plan, so he started barking again.

Charlie *must* have been able to hear us. I think everyone in the park heard us. We were all shouting like crazy.

'Harry, that's enough,' said Mum crossly. How rude. 'Tom, he's wandered off, and it's dark. We need to find him.'

'Yep, agreed,' said Dad. 'I'll check ahead. You guys go back to the main path in case he's gone that way, and I'll meet you by the playing fields.'

He started walking away from us. 'He'll be fine, I'll find the little chicken giblet in no time,' he called over his shoulder.

'Come on Harry,' said Mum, pulling me to my feet and taking Tuppence's lead.

'Where is he? Is he lost?'

'No, he's just… gone ahead. He's fine.'

'Ow, you're squashing me!' Mum was holding my hand tightly.

'Sorry sweetie. Charlie! Charlie! Charlie!' she called as we walked. But the only reply was the scrunch of our feet on the path.

'Excuse me!'

A big man with an enormous black dog, at least five times larger than Tuppence, was walking towards us. He stopped, although he didn't have much choice as Mum stood right in the middle of the path.

'Have you seen my little boy? Blue jacket, yellow wellies, three years old, umm, Harry, help me out here… '

'Crazy hair?' I suggested.

'Yes, curly hair.'

'No, sorry love, I haven't. How long has he been lost?'

Mum and I both spoke at once.

'Ten minutes,' she said.

'Ages and ages,' I said.

'My husband is searching for him that way,' said Mum, pointing up the path. 'But he could have gone down any of these little routes.'

The man reached into his coat pocket and pulled out his mobile phone. 'OK, hold on a second, perhaps we can find him.'

'You said Charlie wasn't lost!' I whispered to Mum.

'He's maybe a bit lost. But we'll find him soon, I promise,' she whispered back.

'Nigel, it's Gary again,' said the man into his phone. 'Are you still in the park?'

He raised his eyebrows at us and gave us a grin. 'Splendid. Now then, we have a bit of a 'situation' here.' The man said 'situation' like it was a special word with a train in the middle: sit-*choo*-ay-shun.

'Need your assistance. Little boy gone AWOL down in Minton Woods, by the football pitches. Not much intel to go on: three years old, blue jacket, curly hair. I'm with the mother now.'

The man gave us another grin. 'Good question, I'll ask.'

He put his hand over his phone. 'What's his name?'

'Charlie,' said Mum.

'Cheeky Charlie,' I added. 'With yellow wellies.'

The man nodded and repeated it into his phone, although he didn't say the cheeky bit which I thought was silly because he might find the wrong boy.

'Yep, Roger that Nigel, I knew you'd be up for it. I'll cut up from the south with Bubbles. You double back from there, and recce the northern territory. We'll rendezvous in twenty by the goal posts.'

That's a weird way to talk, I thought. For starters, what's his friend's name – Roger, or Nigel? And who's Bubbles?

It turns out I must have said that last bit out loud because the man pointed at his huge black dog. Bubbles had draped himself across the man's feet, ignoring us and Tuppence.

'OK, over and out.' The man slipped his phone back into his pocket. 'Heel, Bubbles, we've got work to do!' The dog got reluctantly to his feet. He didn't seem keen.

'Don't you worry, Miss, we'll have your sprog back in his scratcher before lights out,' he said to

Mum. 'He's probably building a den somewhere.'

What was he was talking about? Sprog? Scratcher? Lights out? I looked into the trees; there was almost no difference between the branches and the black sky. And it was certainly a funny time to make a den.

'I'll search back up towards the road,' he said, 'and my wingman is searching in the other direction. Head back to the playing fields with the boy and wait there.'

'Boy?' I said. 'My name's Harry, I'm not a boy.'

The man frowned. 'Harry? Funny name for not-a-boy.'

Grr. Why did everyone have to be so rude today? 'Well Bubbles is a silly name for –' I started.

'Harry, not now. Besides, I'm not waiting anywhere,' said Mum unexpectedly. 'My son is lost, and I need to find him. Come on Harry. But thank you for your help.'

'Suit yourself. Still, no man left behind and all that. Right Bubbles, let's do this!'

The big man took a few steps along the path and turned sharp left. There wasn't a path, so he crashed straight through the bushes, bish bash bosh, repeating 'Charlie! Charlie! Charlie!' in the same voice like a mad robot. Bubbles followed after, still looking like he'd rather curl up in front of the telly.

'He was a nice man,' I said, 'at least until the end bit.'

'Yes, very… helpful,' said Mum. 'Come on, let's go.' And she gripped my hand again and pulled me forward along the path, with Tuppence trotting along by my side.

We walked fast. Mum didn't say anything, except to call out Charlie's name. Other people were calling, too: men's voices, in different directions, out of the darkness. The wood seemed enormous.

We reached the main path without meeting anybody else. Mum pulled us to a stop and called Dad. She didn't say hello.

'Have you found him?' Mum pulled me closer while she listened.

'What did the police say, when will they get here?'

The police? OK, this was serious.

'I'm back by the playing fields, where the path

turns in.' Mum scuffed the ground with her foot, backwards and forwards, backwards and forwards.

'OK, we'll meet them by the gate. Yes, I'm sure you're right, but it's late. I'm worried. Bye.'

'Mummy, is Charlie lost now? What has happened to him? Why are the police coming?'

'I don't know, love.' Mum started walking, taking us straight across the playing field towards the road. 'I'm sure he's fine, we just can't find him, and the police will help us.'

We reached the gate without talking. I climbed up to the top and leaned over, looking up the road. Tuppence stuck his head through the bars while Mum sent messages on her phone.

We didn't have to wait long.

'Mummy! Police!'

Flashing blue lights were racing towards us down the hill. 'Why don't the police have their nee-naws on?'

Mum didn't answer.

The police car stopped at the kerb next to us. I stared for a bit too long at the blue flashing lights and nearly fell off the gate.

'Don't move, Harry,' she said. And she climbed up onto the gate like me, and jumped right over –

like a kangaroo or something. She never does that normally; she always tells me to open the gate instead.

Mum ran across and leaned in through the car window. Mum pointed a lot back towards the wood and at one point I heard her say, 'Only three. He's only three.'

She stood up, and the police car drove off, really fast, with the flashing lights back on. In fact it started so fast its wheels did a bit of a skid. Although still no nee-naws.

'Where are they going, Mummy?'

'To help us find Charlie,' she said.

Mum's phone rang. 'Yep, they just arrived,' she told Dad. 'They're heading round to the main gate in case he went that way, and another car is on the way to start looking from our side.'

Mum chewed her nails. That's another thing she tells me not to do. 'No, I've still got Harry with me, and the dog. We'll walk back towards you. Can you give Hannah a bell, get her to come down and pick Harry up?'

'No!' I said. I did *not* want to go home.

Mum looked at me and put her finger on her lips. 'OK, we'll meet you on the path.' She paused.

'I hope you're right. He's just… so small. Yes, I love you too.' Mum made a funny noise, a bit like a hiccup and a sniff at the same time.

As she turned towards me, the yellow from the streetlight shone on her face. She was crying. In a moment of time, a speck as tiny as glitter, the excitement disappeared. I was frightened.

We were half way back across the playing fields when Dad met us: he appeared out of the night, put his arm around Mum, and we walked on towards the woods. They talked quietly. Tuppence snuffled around, jiggling and jerking the lead.

As we got near, men and women were shouting Charlie's name. Between the words there was almost nothing, only the cracking of branches. A bright white light flickered through the trees – someone with a torch. I wished I had a torch.

Mum's phone buzzed with a message.

'That's Hannah,' she said. 'She's down by Minton Lane. I'll cut through with Harriet and she'll take her back to her house until we get home.'

'No!' I said again.

'Not now, muffin,' said Dad. 'You go with Hannah and we'll be right along with Charlie very soon.'

'But –'

'No buts,' said Mum, like she meant it. 'That's what needs to happen. Come on.' She turned to Dad. 'I'll call you.'

Dad nodded.

'Find him, love.' Mum was speaking quietly.

Dad nodded again. 'I will. I promise.'

They kissed quickly and Dad headed off around the playing fields. Mum, Tuppence and I entered the woods on a different path, the one that goes straight through the middle and out to the lane.

This path is quite narrow, but it has lampposts on it with pale circles of yellow light. They're quite far apart. Between them it was darker than ever.

We weren't talking, and I had to do little skips to keep up. Tuppence bounced with excitement, running ahead and out into the bushes as far as his lead would let him.

We came to a crossroads where our path crossed a smaller one. Mum walked straight on, but Tuppence had another idea. He did a full-speed run down the side path, so hard that the clip came undone on his collar. Before I realised, I was holding an empty lead.

'Tuppence!' I shouted. 'Mummy, Tuppence has run off!'

Mum turned back. 'We haven't got time for this, Harry. Hannah is waiting for you.'

'But we can't leave Tuppence. Look, he's there!'

A little way down the path, Tuppence sat neatly, looking at us and barking.

Mum didn't say anything to stop me so I ran towards him. But as soon as I bent down to attach the lead he ran off again.

'Tuppence, come back!' I shouted as I ran after him.

'Harry!' shouted Mum. This story involves a lot of shouting, I'm sorry about that, but it's the way that it happened.

She followed me as I zoomed through the trees. When I'm running I take little steps and do jumps but Mum runs like a galumphing, grunting elephant. And since there wasn't room for two on the narrow path she ran behind me.

This path didn't have any lights, but I saw where

the gaps were between the bushes. Sometimes I spotted the hairy white end of Tuppence's tail whenever he slowed down.

We turned a corner. I stopped and Mum crashed into the back of me, grabbing my shoulders and nearly pushing me over.

'He's disappeared!'

'We're going to have to leave him,' said Mum. 'He's bound to make his own way back.'

But just then Tuppence started barking from somewhere nearby.

'We have to get him,' I said. 'He's not even our dog. I think he's through there.' I pointed at a gap between a tree and a bush: not really a path at all.

'One more minute,' said Mum, 'and we're heading back, like it or not.'

Before she'd even finished, I pushed through the gap. The barks were getting louder and there was something else: the sound of water.

I swerved through the trees and bushes. Once I took a wrong turning and the barks and the water started to get quieter. So I pushed back past Mum so she wouldn't stop me and turned a different way. The right way.

'Harry!' cried Mum. She sounded quite upset.

'Enough's enough!'

'I can nearly see Tuppence!' I called back. We had reached the muddy stream, the one we had found when we went for a walk with Dad.

Except that it didn't look the same, not at all. On that walk we'd found a dribble of water running down the middle, so small that you could make a dam with one foot.

Not any more. The stream was about as wide as my bed, and half way up the sides of the ditch. The water rippled and splashed as it surged around the rocks and the stuck logs.

I couldn't get over the stream. There was a little path along the bank so I chose that way, around a bend.

In front of me a big, dark shape blocked the way: a square of blackness. A doggy shape was outlined against it: Tuppence. He was sitting still, staring down at the stream. His barks weren't so quick now, but they kept coming: Bark! Bark! Bark!

I suddenly realised where I was: alongside the bridge. The same bridge we'd stood on in the summer. It's right over a little waterfall thingy that Dad called a weir, but Charlie called a weird instead. Charlie had cried because there wasn't enough water to play pooh sticks. So we'd climbed down beside it and squiggled our feet in the mud.

Now though, the water rushed under the narrow bridge. It wasn't exactly a roar, but it certainly didn't sound friendly.

'Got you!' I huffed as I ran up to Tuppence. I grabbed his collar to stop him getting away. He wagged his tail.

Mum arrived, puffing a bit. 'We must get back. Hannah will be waiting for us and so is Dad and the police are looking and –'

'Mummy!' She doesn't like it when I interrupt her. But that was strange. Yes, there it was again. It sounded like an animal had hurt itself. 'Listen!'

'I can't hear anything,' said Mum, and sure enough, the sound had stopped. But it had definitely been coming from under the bridge.

I did little tippy steps forward, like you do when you get out of bed in the middle of the night and you don't want to bang your toes on the dressing up box. I was walking towards the stream so I didn't want to get this wrong. I reached out with one hand and felt the rough, cold bricks of the bridge wall. Tuppence stood up and pushed himself against my ankles, making a whimpering noise.

There – the noise again.

'Harriet, let me through, this is dangerous,' said Mum.

'It's OK, I'm being careful.' I was super-scared. Being super-scared makes you super-careful. But I had to find out who – or what – was under that bridge.

With my toes I felt the edge of the bank. I looked over the edge. It was blackety-black straight ahead and not much better straight down, either: only the occasional reflection on the water, the swooshing, sloshing sound and Tuppence whimpering by my feet.

'Harry, get back,' said Mum. 'We're wasting time.'

I waited another minute, but... nothing. I turned to climb up the bank to the bridge but I tripped over Tuppence, invisible in the darkness. It was my second fall of the day, and I landed on my side in the slippery mud. I screamed.

'Harry!' Mum shouted, as she slid down towards me. 'Hold on!'

I tried to push myself to my feet but my knees slipped on the leaves. First one leg slipped over the edge into the blackness, then the other.

'Mummy, I'm falling!'

I dropped down into the river. Except my feet didn't hit the water. Instead they landed on a muddy ledge that ran along the river bank, just above the swirls and splashes. This ledge was only as wide as an exercise book so it was impossible to know it was there from the edge. But I was now standing on it, trying not to slip into the water, screaming at Mum to help me.

Down here the noise terrified me; a sound that filled your head, bullying and pushing, making sure that no other noises squeezed in. Tuppence was standing on the edge above me, his doggy mouth moving silently.

Mum leaned down and I grabbed both her hands. She pulled and pulled, but my hands were muddy and slippery and I was finding it hard to hold on. Half way up the bank, my right hand slipped right out of hers. I twizzled round so I was facing the bridge.

And that's when I saw it. A flash of something in the darkness, something that shouldn't be there. I yanked my other hand out of Mum's grip and slid back onto the ledge.

She waved her hands at me, her eyes open wide, and shouted something. But I pointed under the bridge and started to edge my way towards it.

The closer I got, the more certain I became. The ledge sloped down to steps that vanished into the rushing water. And there, in the darkest corner of the darkest bridge of the darkest woods in the world, sat Charlie.

His bright yellow wellies were on the bottom step, water splashing over them. He had buried his head in his lap, facing the other way.

'Charlie!' I yelled, using every voice muscle I had.

Charlie's head shot up. His mud-streaked face shone in the darkness, and even from here I could see the tears running down his cheeks. He didn't say anything; he just held out both hands towards me, his eyes wide and his lip quivering.

Mum moved so fast it made me blink. (It didn't really, I'm the best at not blinking, but I read that in a story once.) She lowered herself down onto the ledge and picked Charlie up by the armpits.

As she did it, one of Charlie's wellies got caught on the step, and fell off into the stream.

'Mummy!' I shouted, and pointed.

Mum didn't try to shout back; she shook her head and held Charlie under one arm, like a bag of shopping. I watched the yellow boot swirl off down the stream, into the darkness.

Mum put her free hand under my bottom and shoved me back up onto the bank. It took her a bit more panting to climb up herself without letting go of Charlie. I held his hand and felt the shudders running through his body. His hand was icy cold.

Together we climbed up onto the bridge and walked back towards the lights: me first, then Mum carrying Charlie, and finally Tuppence who wasn't even back on the lead. At least the dog was a happy chappy again, all snuffles and waggly tail.

Guess how we got home. Go on, guess. OK so you may be right, but you'll have to wait and see because I'm not telling you on this page.

So as we walked, Mum called Dad and Dad

called the police, and we all met up by the gate on the lane.

There were other people there too, more and more of them appearing all the time, all smiling and laughing. Gary was there with Bubbles, and his mate Nigel turned up, too – or was it Roger? Either way he was the exact opposite of Gary: a tiny man with a teeny-weeny, pink-eared dog that wouldn't sit still. Guess the name of the dog? Tiger.

A policewoman bent down to talk to me, but her walkie-talkie started crackling so loud it hurt my ears. She twiddled it with her fingers to make it go quiet.

'You must be Harriet,' she said to me. 'I saw you earlier by the gate, when I was talking to your Mummy.'

I opened my mouth, but nothing came out. I wanted to tell her all about it, but for some reason my voice wasn't working.

'I've heard all about how brave you were,' she said. 'It's a good job you and your dog are such good detectives.'

'It's not my dog,' I whispered.

'Isn't it?' she said. 'Well you make a superb

team. Maybe one day you'll have a four-legged partner of your own.' What a good idea! And my birthday *is* coming up... was this the right time to ask?

I looked over at Mum, sitting in the back of the police car. She was still cuddling Charlie, still holding him like she was afraid somebody might take him away from her. I'd ask for a dog a bit later.

Dad, who had been shaking everybody's hand, came over and put his arm round my shoulders. 'Let's go home, sugar plum,' he said.

'Can we give you a lift?' said the policewoman.

My heart did a little jump with excitement. 'I should coco,' Dad said.

'That means yes please,' I said to the policewoman, who smiled and pointed to the car.

'Any chance of the blues and twos?' said Dad as he got into the front. 'That means the nee-naws,' he whispered back to me, 'I learned that from the telly.'

'Not without another emergency, I'm afraid. And I think we've had enough of those for one night,' she said. She looked in the car mirror at Charlie, sandwiched between me and Mum.

He'd stopped crying now, but he was still only whispering.

And so that's how we got home, in a police car. Tuppence couldn't come, perhaps because he had muddy paws, so Nigel-or-Roger walked him home and apparently Tuppence quarrelled with Tiger all the way back. Maybe Tuppence was showing off about his search-and-rescue skills. Nobody likes a show-off.

As we got out, Dad walked round to say goodbye to the policewoman and Mum opened the front door. 'Wave goodbye, kids,' said Dad. And as we waved the policewoman turned on the blue lights and did a little 'whoop-whoop' on the siren. Dad gave her the thumbs up and closed the door.

A bit later, after we had got changed into our jimjams, we cuddled together on the sofa with Tuppence curled up at our feet.

'I don't understand. Why didn't you shout, darling?' Mum asked Charlie.

'I did, a bit,' said Charlie in an almost-normal

voice. 'But nobody came. And Daddy said he give me 10p if I stay quiet.'

'What?' spluttered Dad. 'I never –' he stopped. 'Ah. Yes, I did.' He turned to Mum, who had her 'I-want-an-explanation' face on, the one where she raises her eyebrows and tilts her head to one side. 'I can explain, I promise.'

'And explain you will,' she said. 'Right, bedtime for *everyone*. Charlie, Harry, Tom: upstairs. Tuppence: bed.'

Tuppence dragged himself to his feet and tip-tapped off to the kitchen. And faster than it takes to watch an episode of Peppa Pig, we were all in bed and fast asleep.

The next morning Mum pulled the covers off me and started talking. How rude.

'Where's Charlie?' she said. 'He's not in his bed. Where is he?'

I didn't say anything: what could I say, I'd just woken up.

'Tom, where's Charlie?' She leaned over the banisters. 'Is he down with you?'

'I think you'd better come and take a look down here,' Dad said. He didn't mean me, but this sounded interesting. So I jumped off my bunk bed onto the bean bag – that's my special trick – and ran down behind Mum.

'Is he OK?' said Mum.

'He's more than OK,' said Dad as he led us through into the kitchen. 'Have a butchers at this.'

At first we couldn't see him, but Mum started laughing and pointed. Because there was Charlie, curled up and fast asleep with his arms around Tuppence in the big red basket. As snug as a bug in a rug.

'That's it,' Mum said. 'I can't take it. No way am I letting you lot leave the house ever again.'

And she pulled Dad and me towards her and held us close for a long, long time.

Read on...for free!

For children: so did you enjoy my stories? If you did, that awesome Cheeky Charlie Mini-Book is waiting for you – completely free!

It's all about me and Charlie at a music festival. Expect smelly toilets and a man with incredibly hairy feet. It's a humdinger, which is another Dad word for excellent, and he's still right.

So find a grown-up, get them to read the bit underneath. Don't wait!

Adults: I sometimes send out emails about new Charlie stories that are about to be published, other books that I'm working on, and stuff I think you'll like. I don't do it often, and I try to make them as useful as possible. Sometimes even funny. As a thank you, I'll send you *Festival* – a seven-chapter Charlie Mini-book. It's packed with fun and it'll do enough bedtimes to last until the weekend. After that, I'm afraid you're on your own.

Sound good? To get it, just sign up for my emails at **matwaugh.co.uk/freeminibook** now.

One last thing...

I need your help.

Every review of Charlie on Amazon makes it more likely that other parents and children will discover him, just like you've done. Here's one written about book one:

'You simply have to read this rodingly funny book! Its menacing and egkillicent!'

Now I don't even know what 'egkillicent' means. But I'm just happy that this reader took a moment to let others know what they thought.

So parents and children: please nip over to Amazon and rate this book. I can't wait to hear from you.

Mat

Also by Mat Waugh

Cheeky Charlie

From Amazon, or free eBook: matwaugh.co.uk

Cheeky Charlie: King of Chaos (Book 3)

Available soon – subscribe to hear about it first!

Cheeky Charlie: He Didn't Mean It (Book 4)

Available Spring 2018.

Cheeky Charlie: Festival

Free for subscribers. **matwaugh.co.uk/freebook**

Coming soon for older children:

The Fun Factor

In a remote village, the stuff everyone loves is disappearing by the day. First to go is the internet. Next up: phones, pizzas, TV channels and even the dishwasher. Twelve-year-old Thora and her friends struggle to see what's so fun about the good old days, but soon discover they're guinea pigs in a decidedly high-tech social experiment…

About Mat Waugh

I'm a father of three young girls. I'm often tired. These two things are connected.

I live in Tunbridge Wells, which is a lively, lovely town in the south east of England.

Small boys scare me – they do too much running, and not enough drawing. But I'm petrified by the thought of three teenage girls.

When I was seven I wrote to Clive King. He's the author of my favourite childhood book, *Stig of the Dump*, which is about a caveman who lives in a house made out of rubbish. I asked Clive if there was going to be a sequel, but he said no.

I've had lots of writing and editing jobs, but mostly for other people.

I forgot: I also had a crazy year when I thought I wanted to be a teacher. But then I found out how hard teachers work, and that you have to buy your own biscuits. So I stopped, and now I just visit schools to eat theirs and talk to children about stories.

That letter from Clive King gave me the idea that I could write my own stories, but I could never find the right moment. So I waited until I had children and had no spare time at all. If you want something done, ask a busy person.

I started writing about Charlie because I want to make children laugh, without making the grown-ups sigh, or cry. Grown-ups will know what I mean.

I'm also writing books for slightly older children. The stories are a bit more scary, and there aren't as many bottom jokes.

One more thing: I love hearing from readers. Funny stuff, silly stuff, serious stuff. Any kind of stuff, in fact. If that's you, then please get in touch.

✉ mail@matwaugh.co.uk
www.matwaugh.co.uk

Or, if you're old enough:

f facebook.com/matwaughauthor
🐦 twitter.com/matwaugh

31006663R00074

Printed in Great Britain
by Amazon